THE

KINGS
HEAD

THE
KINGS HEAD

KELLY FROST

atlantic · *fiction*

First published in hardback in Great Britain in 2025 by Atlantic Books,
an imprint of Atlantic Books Ltd.

1 2 3 4 5 6 7 8 9

A CIP catalogue record for this book is available from the British Library.

Hardback ISBN: 978 1 80546 238 5
EBook ISBN: 978 1 80546 239 2

Printed and bound by CPI (UK) Ltd, Croydon CR0 4YY
Atlantic Books
An imprint of Atlantic Books Ltd
Ormond House
26–27 Boswell Street
London
WC1N 3JZ

www.atlantic-books.co.uk

And make your chronicle as rich with praise
As is the ooze and bottom of the sea
With sunken wrack and sumless treasuries

—William Shakespeare, *Henry V*

Tony, 2017

The handwriting looks like hers. 'CLOSING SUNDAY' in a crude, blocky, *go-away* font that's as childish as it is authoritative. I stare at the letters, heart thrumming, and wait for them to come alive, or perhaps for her to appear behind the glass door with that silly smile, ink all up her wrists from the writing. Instead, the letters sit there, dull on the paper. Taped to the door. Flapping in the wind. And behind the notice, suddenly the puzzled face of a man looms in the glass, wiping away my vision of Harry.

This man wants to exit – but he wants me to get out of the way first, so we've got a stalemate, because I can't go in until he comes out. He relents, eventually, pushing out and past me, before diving into a halal shop across the road.

I enter, thinking the notice must be a mistake. Or that the owners are going on holiday, like in France, where the restaurateurs close their doors for two weeks to sun themselves in the Riviera. Or an error on my part, and

I've come to the wrong Kings Head on the wrong corner. Or maybe it's just a prank by local kids. Anything but the truth.

We did worse in our day, getting ourselves banned from half the cinemas this side of the Bridge, sometimes for good reasons but more often not. I still blame Harry for getting us chucked out of the Astoria, among other things. Who steals a bloody projector? She smacked it down on that corner table like a relic while we gathered around and asked her why the *bloody hell* she'd done it. Had she done it? *Did you?* I asked, shaking her body outside the police station. She just smirked and wouldn't say.

It's becoming harder to see her in the rickety chair where a man now sits, his haunches spilling out over the sides. Same old carpet, popcorn walls, but the jackpot machines click and flip around their dollar signs in the background, blaring bingo applause after applause. The six-or-so beer-faced customers fix their eyes on the football match on the flatscreen on the wall. The rhythm of this place now completely different, hostile to memories.

'What's going on?' I ask the kid behind the bar, waving towards the notice on the door. He looks up, thumb poised over his phone screen, itching to continue scrolling. It's the same bartender as last year, not even twenty, polite but punkish, with studs in his ears and nose, and a thin black tattoo of a spiky heartbeat line on his neck where the pulse thrums. Usually, he entertains the idea of us, like cats with wool, as long as it's convenient. His eyes scan me up and down with the disinterested look of a kid considering a museum exhibit. I'm long past expecting people to recognize me, and, of course, he has no idea who I am, or was.

'What do you think?' He has clocked what I'm referring to, but returns to his phone. 'Closing means closing.'

'Yes, but… permanently?'

He sighs loud enough to make it clear I'm interrupting.

'You see those houses there,' he points out the back window to a row of shining white terraced houses, their frosted-glass doors embossed with obnoxiously small numbers written as words – *number one, number two, number three.* A block of squat sandstone faces them from the other side of the road, the rectangular green sign and meaningless crest marking them as council flats. A few of us used to live on that street, in buildings long since gone. 'Not the council flats, the posh white houses.' I nod. 'Well, they want to build more of them. Some foreign investor owns half the street now… and the pub, as of last week. I saw him a few days ago, getting out of a Bentley. Bodyguards. The whole thing.' Excitement shines in his eyes. 'Look, I probably shouldn't tell you this, and it's not just because I've already got another job, but… there's ten other pubs just like this one that you can drink in. *Better* ones, probably. It makes no difference to you, does it?'

'No,' I say. 'No difference.'

I order a cranberry juice, and focus on his thin, pale hands as he shuffles three ice cubes into the glass. I want to burst and tell him that there's definitely not ten others like it, not even one, but I swallow the stubborn dread and go to wait for the others at the corner table, where I used to sit with Harry and laugh at men like that.

I know the reunion will be a waste of time. It always is. We had sunk that wasted youth – gone too soon and all that – to yesteryear because that's where it belonged; it was done for a reason, finished, *signed, sealed, delivered.* Au revoir. So long. Farewell. And still we find ourselves in the same place every year, on the same day in November, where we insist on dredging up those days again – anchor days at the end of long chains, lost at the bottom of foggy seas. We cease for a moment, before our muscles finally seize up, and take the time to rerun our old flicks on the table among the napkins and glasses. The leg flicks, finger flicks, knife flicks, all of them dragged there, kicking or screaming, as if it made a difference. As if it would make them stay, make them eternal.

Not long after the millennium, someone suggested we start these reunions – although there wasn't much union left to re, with most of us splattered about the country.

Time folded strangely in the months after the world was supposed to end; nostalgia was becoming fashionable, or maybe the past was simply at arm's length, a safe distance to reach out and stroke. The careful scoping notice in the *Islington Gazette* was like a voice calling out from the past:

> *I was wondering if you can put in your paper that we are planning a reunion for all girls who were members of our old Highbury and Finsbury Park gangs, in the 1950s and 1960s. The place is The Kings Head from 5 p.m. until late on 12th November.*

It was waiting for me in my dressing room under the soft, brown ring of a coffee cup. Someone's left a news-paper cutting for Toni Adams, I was told. *Someone needs to be cut*, Harry had said outside the cinema, as we all hung on her lips. My mouth went dry as the assistant clacked away, leaving me with 12th November.

The date shook loose all those hues from the past – the girls faltering on the grass like a fallen cloud, a crunch of bottle-glass, two screams, a knife stilettoed in a back, the hand it came from clenching air. All too real and not nearly real enough.

A few of us answered the call, keen to return to the place where we made memories and the memories made us. Proximity was the antidote, we were sure – the chance for our chatter to coax out the past from where it hid within the walls. The outsides of our lives becoming blank and irrelevant, as yesterday came into focus. Only we knew these particular shades of fear, the precise pigments that screamed in our nerves, comparing scars like trading cards. Too-sharp visions that made us wince. When the reunions were over, our fingers trembled into the late evenings, as we returned to our kitchen tables and our children and our husbands, putting back on the loose jobs and lives that we had gathered around ourselves.

Seven or eight turned to five or six turned to three or four, dropping like flies. The impermanence made us bitter as the memories wore themselves out like tape, and this building soon became the only evidence that we had ever existed, in a city that could sneeze us off without a trace. If carpets could hold memories, then the patterns of our footsteps would sing out in the blood-red paisley. The faux-mahogany tables and chairs cling tight to the echoes of those tear-ups and trashings, the odd hugs and collisions. Cut the walls and they bleed our old laughter.

ONE

1957

Tony had misplaced the balls – both of them. The other girls were livid, but Tony, swaying as she shut the front door behind her, was too drunk to care.

'Come on, then, where did you last see them?' Saint demanded, swatting Tony's blazered arm, looking at the watch ticking away on Tony's wrist. Less than an hour until the football match. The wind shifted the dried leaves, skittering them around their ankles. Tony pulled the hip flask to her lips for another gulp. '*Think*, Tone, for God's sake. Are they somewhere in your flat?' Saint looked up to the top-floor window.

'Prob-ly not,' Tony said, shrugging.

'What about the park? Did you leave them there last week? In the hole near the gate?'

Tony shrugged again.

Leave it, Saint, the other girls chorused. *She couldn't tell her arse from her elbow.*

Saint threw up both hands in defeat.

'Alright, alright. I give up. It's not my bleeding fault she's drunk for the Sunday football match, or that there's no balls. But if the Kings lose, I'm blaming you.' She started off down the street, the others gathering behind her.

'*She* would fix it… if she was here,' Leslie nodded, head bobbing up and down.

'Well, she's not,' Jackie snapped back. Leslie punched her twin's bicep; Jackie punched back, ever in unison. The twins were identical in both their features – with the same face shape, eye shape, sweep of home-permed brown curls – and their clothing choices. They wore the same scarf tied with the same knot, the same blazer and pin, trousers rolled to the same height above the ankle. It was uncanny (*bloody creepy,* Tony sometimes said), but neither of them cared. Instead, they revelled, in their own ways, in the security of sameness.

The terraced houses rose around them like greying, unsightly weeds, casting the streets into shadow-light nearly-darkness. Through a gentle wishwash of Sunday-afternoon strollers, the Kings walked to the Dent, a burnt-down carcass of a building that had once been a laundrette. On last year's Guy Fawkes Night, a firework had gone astray and hurtled into the terrace. The fire that followed forged a new spot for the youth of North London to congregate. Since then, it had been left as it was, and life moved on around the street's hollow – a permanent gap, undented by time. Piles of dust and rubble formed large, unraked mole-hills, and the charred timbers caused shadows to criss-cross and lace the dusty floors and remaining walls. Half-wasted rafters invited brave climbers to test them: cracked beams showed the results. The Dent didn't look much out of place, with the war still writ large on the streets. Indents in pavements were the echoes of bombs; three stone steps and half a railing leading nowhere.

As the Kings milled around, kicking mounds of caked ash, chatting, filling the silent wreck, another one rushed in: Bert, breathless and blasting out words.

'Have you heard?'

'Heard what?' Saint said, snapping up her head.

'She's back.'

'She *is*?' The twins clambered around each other to reach Bert, who wore the attention of fresh gossip like a cloak over her plainness.

'I've *seen* her.'

'Where?' Saint placed a hand on Bert's shoulder, her eyes darting around, half-expecting someone to jump out of the shadows.

'Just... *around*, you know. Like, earlier. Outside the arcade near Lennox. She looks... different.'

'Different how?' Jackie asked.

'New suit, new hairdo, the whole works. It's short and stiff, all put up and permed, with black slacks and jacket, and the shirt with the high collar that Les was eyeing up on the Row. It must have cost a fortune, even marked down. I don't know where she's got the money.'

'She's really back?' Saint breathed out something deeper than relief. She held a shaking hand to her forehead, pushing back a curled fringe of dirty blonde hair, re-arranging the wire-rimmed spectacles on her nose, as she let the thought intoxicate her:

Harry is back.

Saint remembered the feeling of Harry's approving glance, her lip curling upwards. To have Harry agree with something you said was a rush like no other. Everything else became irrelevant. The girls clustered around the idea of Harry, entranced: it was loyalty in its purest form, awe distilled.

Bert continued, spurred on by the spotlight, 'She even said that she's got a plan for the football match… she wants to mess the Seven Sisters around.' She paused. 'Harry wants their turf.'

'You mean *our* turf,' Jackie butted in.

'Why haven't I heard anything about this?' Saint asked. 'Why didn't she come to me? If she—'

'How long's she been out, then?' Tony interrupted,

springing up from where she was perched on a heap of bricks.

'A couple days. Since Friday, I suppose.' Bert crossed her arms.

'Cor, two months in that hole.'

'I know, but there's no getting around the fact that...' Bert looked up from the clump of rubble she was trying to crumble with her foot. The others waited for her to complete the sentence. 'Well, the fact that it was her bleeding fault she went away in the first place.' The clump broke apart, wind tugging at the wisps of brick dust.

The Kings stilled.

Tony threw the hip flask to the floor and shoved Bert square in the chest.

'Take that back.' She was wobbly on her feet already. It was only four in the afternoon; plenty of night remained for drinking away. 'It was *not* her fault. It just wasn't.' The others rolled their eyes: Tony defending her Harry, with a loyalty blind to logic. How many times had she told them about the day Harry chose *her* to be a King: their disagreement, the cricket bat behind the shed, the blood in Harry's teeth? Repeating it with the cadence of a prayer.

'Bert's right,' Saint smirked. 'You don't get off lightly for coshing an old woman and locking toddlers in a bedroom, and then nicking half the candlesticks. She should have been more careful – it was stupid.'

'She *was* careful. Don't you get it? It was *them* that grassed her up.' Tony turned to Saint. She grabbed her collar, scrunching the starch in her fist. Silence descended like a shot fowl to the ground.

It broke when a pack of young men rounded the corner in a sprint and skidded to a pause. Dark-skinned and wide-eyed, the four of them stared curiously at the girls in their slacks and blazers. Girls dressed like boys, rough like boys, wrestling like boys.

'Oi, what's your problem?' Bert shouted at them. No one replied, their lungs beaten out of breath. The shortest had a cut on his forehead that he touched, looking at the blood on his fingertips. He watched one drip hit the floor, as if wondering how it got there.

'They'll be right behind,' another whispered to the tallest.

'Look, you can see us here, can't you? Move on.' Tony crossed her arms. Still, no reply. Her eyes narrowed. 'Who are you lot, anyway? We're hanging about here, can't you see?' Tony stepped closer to the tallest, puffing out her chest. She was tall, lanky, but her eyeline only skimmed his chin. 'Where're you from anyway?'

He grinned, teeth gleaming. A small chuckle escaped through them and he shook his head.

'Whadcoat Street,' the bleeding one piped up in a Caribbean accent.

'Is that right?' Tony arched her eyebrow. Everyone knew Whadcoat: a smoking clutter of a street, with cobbles of rooms, forgotten houses with rotting bricks, ripe for demolition. All of its residents had been born in different time zones, it was said.

Tony inched another foot closer, but heavy gravel-crunching from the corner of the Dent stopped her from doing whatever she thought she was about to do. Another gang poured into the lot. The Hackney Hackers: acne-scarred, milk-skinned and sooty, with the sharpest pleats in their suit trousers that she had ever seen.

When the Whadcoat gang saw the Hackers crunch into the Dent, which was now becoming particularly packed, they made a run for it, mowing through the Kings.

Tony, Bert and Saint shot off a chorus of *oi* and *watch it*, flinging their hands at the retreating backs. Their voices were barely audible over the skirmish of Hackers continuing the chase. The boys trampled through the Dent, knocking aside the twins and darting off through the rafters to the alley behind. Some of the Hackers remained, idling in the corner and murmuring to themselves, lighting up cigarettes to pass a minute or two.

'Who's that lot, then?' Tony strode towards the Hackers, raising her voice.

Marcus, the taller one, separated himself from the chat. He walked towards Tony and planted himself in front of her, his body as solid as a marble column. His heavy dapper coat hung down nearly to the floor. The collar, turned up to his ears, licked at his slicked-back hair. He carried himself with the surety of a boy who knew he was handsome – had heard it all his life. He lit a cigarette, slowly, as if even the air waited for him.

'Spit it out, who are they, Marcus?' Saint pushed forwards. Marcus pulled the smoke deep into his lungs, enjoying making the Kings wait.

'Some new kids, just moved here, who think they can steal on our turf.' He dragged on the cigarette again. 'Not bloody likely. No one steals from the Hackers.'

'They trouble?'

Marcus looked on, vaguely amused.

'Not for you.'

'You roughed one of them up, though.'

'Like I said, he mistook me for someone he could steal from. He struck Tommy over there,' Marcus gestured behind him at a Hacker rubbing on his jaw, 'and I struck him back. It started into a free-for-all, you see, then they ran.' He took time in his words, wafting the air with his large hands. They were blistered and callused from factory work, with flat-topped fingers and stubby nails, and looked strong enough to grab something and never let go. 'It's alright lovely, don't you worry, we'll get them in time.'

Cigarette in his mouth, Marcus pulled away his jacket and revealed a shining pistol pressed against the waistband.

'Where did you get that?'

'A secret.' He grinned, picking tobacco off his lips. 'Where is she, then? Is she back?'

'She's back.' Bert stepped forward, crossing her arms.

'Shame...' Marcus trailed off without continuing the sentence.

'Shame what?'

'Well, when she's around, you lot turn into a load of sexless beasts... who *think* they're a bloody gang...'

'We *are* one.' Tony shoved him. Marcus flicked his cigarette to the ashy ground and grabbed her wrists. The others watched the skin of her forearms turn white.

'It's a shame, I said. A pretty girl like you in a pair of trousers.'

'Let go, Marcus,' Saint urged. Tommy, the bruised Hacker, started laughing, pointing his own pistol towards Saint. 'Stop it!' the twins pleaded. Marcus lowered his face towards Tony's for a kiss, as she squirmed.

The metal lid of a dustbin collided with Marcus's back. He stumbled and fell into the dirt; grey all on his coat, sticking to the wax greasing his hair. The shiny gun had fallen onto the floor and he scrambled to pick it up and shove it back in his belt. Everyone in the Dent looked towards the source of the lid.

Harry. The afternoon sun swirled around her head as she wielded another lid in her hand.

'Marcus, what did I tell you?' She spoke at a volume few could hit – not much more than a whisper, but with more force than a shout. They leaned in to listen, like iron filings pulled towards a magnet. In fact, if gravity made a noise, it might sound something like that voice.

'You're back, I—' Marcus started, but Harry cut in.

'This spot belongs to the Kings. Bugger off.'

Shouts from a distant alley – *we got them, we got them* – drew Marcus's attention and he jutted his chin at the other Hackers as if to say: *let's get out of here.* He pointed towards the girl wielding the dustbin lid.

'Later, Harry.'

She nodded.

'Later.'

The boys scurried off.

The Kings had not seen Harry for over two months. In late August, as the summer had wound to a close, Harry had taken a job as a nanny with a wealthy-enough family in a posh-enough house in Hampstead. She had boasted to her Kings that she planned to work there for a week or two, to gain their trust, and then, before the first wages were distributed, take a few things to pawn and disappear like a leaf in the wind. On her second day in the job, finding her pockets empty and boredom washing through the depths of her empty stomach like a dull wave – as the story went – she took a candlestick to the grandmother's head, closed the door on the toddlers and walked out of the house with a bottle of whisky and pockets full of cash. The police were waiting for her at the end of the street; she evaded them, for a few minutes at least. Officials tried her, prosecuted her, stood her up in front of a row of bespectacled faces, but at the end of the day, because Harry was little more than twenty and a first-time offender (first time caught, more like), she charmed her way into just two months in Holloway and nothing more. No one knew, for the life of them, why she had done it, who had sent the police, and what had gone wrong. Harry was like that, they said – *no one knows what's going on in her head.*

She had heard kids and Kings tell the story from around corners, down alley ends, at the backs of cafés, and she had let them spin the yarn, losing themselves in it. For several days, she had been biding her time, winding through the streets, calculating the most dramatic of entrances.

And after those two months, Harry was back, with the suddenness of a slap. She dropped the dustbin lid to the pavement and stood, hands on her hips, inspecting them. The Kings – *her* Kings – in their Sunday best. The perfect clobber for hanging around bombed-out buildings, these were the suits they wore every day of the week. The tailored outfits people could no longer afford after the war were suddenly all half price – or occasionally nicked – and Sunday suits for the aristocrats became Monday suits for the Kings. Their salaries, underwritten in blistered and chapped fingers from factory assembly lines and cleaning fluids and typewriters, gave them the cash to get the Edwardian clothing, made for others, cut down to fit their skinny bodies – all sleek and smooth around their spiky joints. Sprinkled in faux pearls, jewellery, gaudy yellow-gold brooches, they stood in steel-capped velvet pumps with their long, bony fingers wrapped around cigarette holders, smoking menthols down to the butt, endlessly puffing clouds that hung in the air long after they had moved on, ghostly hints of their presence wherever they went.

Tony, in a white net hat that no one thought fashionable, trumped across the ashy rubble towards Harry. She embraced her, towering over Harry's slight frame. The smell of alcohol emanated from her in waves.

'Too much communion wine, Tone?' Harry said under her breath. When she pulled away, Harry rearranged her high-necked silk shirt, dotted with four pearl buttons. The padded shoulders on her blazer spiked at the edges. She noticed the others marvelling, and smiled: these were the looks she had pictured when she chose the outfit that morning.

'She's only gone and lost the footballs as well, Harry,' Saint snitched. Tony elbowed her lightly, carelessly, in the gut.

'How was it, then? Doing time?' Jackie clamoured.

'Anyone who's anyone serves a bit of time, isn't that right, Harry?' Tony said, her arm still resting gently on Harry's padded shoulder.

'I bet you beat them silly.' Jackie smiled at her cousin. Nearly a year ago, Harry's aunt had asked if the twins could go around with the Kings. One night, aproned, she gripped Harry's shoulder tight and let her eyes speak sincere: *promise me you'll look after them, protect them from the streets; if they have to be out there at all, then it should be with you.* She had spoken like a woman afraid to use her hands; a woman retracted after years spent piling ammunition into crates. Harry had nodded, and Jackie and Leslie – sixteen-going-on-seventeen now, but sprightly little fourteen-year-old things then – had been taught how to kick and punch, nick and swap, nip and duck, throw and defend, and live on the streets all over. It was safer to be in a gang than outside alone.

'Harry, the Sisters have—' Saint began.

'I know.' Harry reached into her blazer for a cigarette, placing it between her lips.

'The turf...'

'I *know*!' Harry snapped. She found her lighter and lit the cigarette, eventually. The others waited for her to do it. She took a deep drag inward. 'I know about everything that goes on in Kings territory, alright? Is this the part where you ask me what I'm going to do about it?'

'Is it?' Saint asked, like an actor who missed their cue. 'Well, you know how I feel about rules.' Saint spoke directly, pleadingly, to Harry, her eyes blinking nervously, eyelashes fluttering on glass. Her small features – beady eyes, a tight little mouth – twitched. The large plasticky white Os that hung from her ears shook when she spoke.

'It was you what made them.' Harry nodded her head, loosening Saint with flattery.

'And when someone breaks them, I suppose I can't help but—'

'—be a saint about it,' Tony completed, sneering.

'We've got to get back at them,' Saint urged, her cheeks flaring red. 'Now if we look at it, our territory is from the Bridge, along Blackstock to the Head, and the park, of course. But the Sisters were stealing silk shirts from a lorry on our side of the Bridge. That's not right, Harry. It's not on.'

'*It's not on*,' Tony mimicked. Saint barely noticed the mock. It wasn't the first time, and certainly wouldn't be the last, that the Kings picked up on her polished turns of phrase or her expensive jewellery, which stood out next to the tacky, costume stuff the rest of the Kings wore. When they called her *posh* and *brainy* and made fun of her for *reading Plato and Shakespeare and all that caper*, she soaked up their comments like a lizard drinking sunlight.

'The point stands, Harry,' Saint continued.

She was right: the map of Finsbury Park was unmathematical but unmessy, divided up with scalpel-sharp accuracy into units of here, there, that bit, your bit, my bit, *don't-come-near-me-or-I'll-kill-you bit*, this road, that road, ours, yours, theirs – a patchwork of streets, billboards and back alleys, each one hard-fought and hard-protected. There were no rule books, no treaties, but everyone knew where territorial lines fell. It was written in the blood stains and the bruised cheeks and the glares of kids clustered on street corners, outside arcades, choking up cinema rows. Fenced in by gangs like the Hackney Hackers and the Guvnors and a smattering of others, the Kings made a claim on their side of the Woodbine Cigarettes Bridge. The other side, the side that made up a large portion of the Seven Sisters Road, belonged to the Cosh Boys, a set of eighteen-year-old pimpled not-quite-men from the estates near Holloway Road. The Coshers fought with the Hackers and the Guvnors, the Coshers fought with whoever fought with them, the Coshers fought with themselves, and now the Coshers fought overseas. Their draft had come in and

all but a lonely two or three had dribbled off to training camps and further afield. Cyprus was the rumour,
although no one knew precisely where Cyprus was.
Somewhere hot, exotic.

In their wake, they left their auxiliaries, the so-called
Seven Sisters – so-called because no one knew what to
call them. The sideliners. The lean-tos. The glorified
girlfriends, Harry called them, which was what the
twenty-or-so Kings scattered around Finsbury Park called
them too. But a week after Harry had disappeared, and
speculation grew that the Sisters had staged the arrest,
they claimed the Bridge and crossed the spat of road
shaded from the stars that separated the two territories.
With the glint of moonlight on blades, they began lifting
packets of cigarettes from the shops, nicking contraband
from lorries. A lip of Kings' territory near the Bridge had
since become the Sisters' – and when the Coshers were
back, it would belong to them too.

'We can't let them have it,' Saint muttered.

'And we won't.' An undercurrent of steel in Harry's
voice. The cigarette was a stub in her fingers now. 'This
side of the Bridge is ours, all of it. And if it's ours, then I
don't see why the Sisters can come and conduct business
here. Now look, it might only be a street or two, a couple
of silk scarves... but come next week, the Seven Sisters
will be in our pub and dancing on our floors and there

won't be a bloody thing we can do about it.' The Kings nodded, breathless in the incoming dusk. 'We'll play the football match—'

'We'll play it?' Tony burst out. 'With *them*. When they *stole* from us. Are you making some sort of joke, Harry?'

'If you'd let me finish...' Harry stared at her. Tony relaxed, uncoiling. 'We'll play for the turf.' She paused. 'All of it.'

'But what if the Sisters win?' Saint asked. 'That's it, that's the Kings done for good. Harry, I can't—'

'They won't win. I guarantee it.'

'Oh, you guarantee it, do you?' Saint shook her head.

The Kings fell silent, waiting on Harry's next word. Tony's fingers itched at her side.

'Really? Nothing? From any of you? I suppose we'd better go, then, if we want to be on time to lose all this turf.' Saint tapped at her watch with a long nail, looking up to the sky. The sun swung towards the horizon with peachy streaks. It would be light for only another hour. Bert and the twins followed her up Blackstock Road towards the park. Tony stayed behind, sloughing some of her showmanship.

'You sure about this?' she asked Harry. 'You've only just got out and—'

'I wouldn't do it if I wasn't sure.' Harry looked ahead at the retreating backs of her Kings. 'Just think about it,

Tone. Losing our streets… we wouldn't be able to look at ourselves in the mirror. And if we lost it all, all that we had, where would we go then?' She continued: 'It's not just for a giggle, Tony, you understand that, right? About this acting tough, this being Kings: it's no good creeping around like the other girls, like you've got no right to be on these streets. We've got every right. Even if we have to settle for only a few of them, unlike the boys, you can't ignore that… that *superior* feeling of confidence you get when you walk down our streets, can you?'

'Don't make it sound so bloody life and death. It doesn't do anyone any good to think like that. In the future, we won't even think about this patch. It'll be ancient history.'

'*I'll* think of it. It's not only a patch, Tone, it's…' Harry trailed off, picked up a rock and threw it at one of the caved-in walls, just to hear the echo. 'Two months.' She shook her head. 'Every day I thought about this.' She pointed to the ground under her feet. 'I thought about how it might slip through your fingers when I wasn't here. I thought about the floor of this place, the beams. You know, the way the sun comes through in the mornings and the moonlight at night. I thought about it like it was already gone, and I knew then I'd rather lose my eyes than lose this place. You know I had nightmares in there? I've never had nightmares before… I saw the

Coshers walking on our streets, stamping you lot into the ground. You were gone and our turf was gone. It was awful.'

'Harry...' Tony stepped towards her, but Harry moved off. She eyed the well-dressed backs of the other Kings who hurtled to the horizon like comets. 'I'm sorry about the turf, Harry, but without you... we didn't know what to do with ourselves.'

'It's alright.' Harry shook her head. 'I shouldn't have gone away.'

'I never got the chance to ask what happened. You say that like you had a choice about going away, but everyone said the Sisters did it—'

'The Sisters aren't that smart,' Harry scoffed. 'But if it's what the Kings think, then let's keep it that way.'

'If it wasn't them, then... are you alright, Harry? They wouldn't let me call or write. It's the longest we've been apart. You *never* get caught, and I mean *never*. I heard some kids talking, saying you were... *unhinged.*'

Harry choked on her own laugh. She turned away from the brewing sunset.

'How long have you known me, Tone?' she asked.

'Well, I couldn't say... long enough.'

'Long enough to trust me when I say I'm fine. I'm happy.'

'You *say* you're happy, but somehow you don't look it.'

'Stop asking me.' Harry's face was firm, chiselled. 'I don't ask about *that*, do I?' Her eyes veered to the hip flask still nestled in ash. She was right; after Harry's example, no one asked about Tony's drinking, her swagger, leer or volatile temper. No one asked Tony why she flinched at loud noises, why she let others turn corners before she did. All they knew was that Tony never talked about the war; and she never talked about wanting to leave Finsbury Park anymore. Her desire for flight had been all shunned – *scared*, some said, out of her earshot – into fight.

'Saint's right, like she always is… we'll be late,' Harry said. 'That's the last time I let you keep the balls.'

'I'm never going to hear the end of that, am I?' Tony laughed, shaking her head, as they started down the street. Ahead, the skinny sinners hurled themselves at the park gates, knocking over dustbins, tipping their hats to policemen on the beat. The plan swirled in Harry's head like the fleecy clouds across what remained of the day's blue sky, teased apart, slowly clomping together. She thought about that evening, she thought about tomorrow and the drinks they would share over their victory, the shouts and dances and celebrations. Tomorrow would be theirs. It felt certain.

Harry wasn't planning on handing over their turf, even if the Kings lost the match.

She looked over protectively at Tony and the rest of her Kings: they were on a need-to-know basis. The made-up wager would provide the much-needed sense of unity that had gone missing during her absence.

Despite herself, she thought of yesterday – and beyond yesterday, to two months ago – and she decided she would never tell them, not even Tony, that she got herself caught. She amused herself with the word *unhinged*, busting open the door on her mind, thinking of that first day with the spoilt toddlers in a gilt-filled room in Hampstead, echoes bounding in her chest as she shouted back at the little red-cheeked screaming monsters.

Her voice had already been hoarse from the night before when Mr George had caught her returning from the streets near midnight, stuffing stolen cigarettes into her pockets, a split lip and a bruised cheek from where the shopkeeper had rushed after her and she fell into the street. Mr George, the old man who lived in the rooms next door, had beckoned her inside. The walls had been thin enough for him to know all the colours of her father's cough at the varying stages of his disease; neighbours stacked too close to each other for comfort. He couldn't help but feel for her, he had said, this girl *still acting out against the world*. He had told her that she was *not a teenager anymore*, which meant *old enough to know better*. He had told her that she was now a daughter and husband to her mother, a father and sibling to her little sister. She had to be all these things she had no idea how to be. The only time she knew for sure was with the Kings, where she was Harry, *their* Harry. She was fearless. Or, at least, others saw her like that and that was enough.

You can't keep torturing your mum like this, he'd said, the old voice breaking. *If you want money, then you need to get employment. You need to look after your family. Otherwise, the only way to look after them is to get yourself as far away from them as you can.*

She had tried employment; the other Kings seemed able to do it, even if she'd heard Tony insist too many times that there were no interesting jobs for girls of their age. As a nipper, Tony had talked about going abroad all the time – now, the ambition flushed all out of her, she cleaned schools, just to sniff at the fluids. Saint typed letters for a literary gentleman. Bert kept houses. When the toddlers screamed, Harry screamed back. Her mind wandered out the window. And her hand reached for the golden candlesticks on the table. And the panic – the sweet panic – rushed into her chest, knotting itself into her lungs and putting down its heels. With no way to shake it out, she took Mr George's advice and closed the door gently on the toddlers (the handle was out of their reach anyway), called the police from the bedroom and walked out of the house – turning back to take the whisky and the notes and coins in the top kitchen drawer, to make the act convincing. She still didn't know why she had done it.

All she knew was that it was good to be back, the king of Kings, larking around with Tony; back in her uniform of gaudy brooches and pumps. She would die before she let this turf – Edie's turf – out of her hands.

TWO

Late 1954

'Tone, repeat Edie's instructions back to me.'

Harry and Tony were crouched, tense, at the end of an alley. Barely sixteen, they had been Kings for not even one year. Looker-uppers, tripping on the heels of the older girls in front.

'The lorry will pull in at ten,' Tony recited. 'The driver will get out and head inside to meet the owner of the shop. That's our chance. Unlatch the back, take as much as we can carry, and when we see them—'

'—we run,' Harry completed the plan like the end of a prayer. God, the father. *Have mercy upon us.* She still remembered how her mother's tears had bled through those words at her father's funeral – and continued to bleed all over unpaid bills on the kitchen table.

Rain started pattering, drifting in the sparse orange streetlights.

'How much longer?' Tony whispered. They were passing a hand-rolled cigarette back and forth, tasting each other on the paper. Harry threw it into the gutter and flipped out the pocket watch Edie had given her. Tony looked over, trying to see the face for herself, before Harry snatched it back into her pocket.

'It should be any minute now.' Harry glanced around, Edie's words from earlier that day looming in her head. She and Tony had nicked from the back of a lorry before, but this was the first time the leader of the Kings had trusted them to go it alone, and she couldn't help but think it was a test. Beside her, Tony's teeth chattered; it was a mild evening.

'What do you call a blue that's not as heavy as all the other blues?' Harry asked.

'What?'

'You heard me.'

'Not a clue, Harry.'

A crunch of wheels rounded the corner. They watched as the lorry pulled up, the driver hopped out and wandered around the cab towards the back door of the shop.

'Light blue.'

'You're an idiot.' Tony smiled.

The driver knocked, the door opened, he went in.

'Go.'

They raced around the corner and down the side street, feet thwacking on the cracked road. Tony looked out, swivelling her neck towards the door, the cab, the mouth of the street, while Harry jumped up and yanked the latch. It opened, revealing riches of dresses before them; evening gowns on racks, boxes of furs and fake pearls. The two began grabbing at what they could find, stuffing trinkets in their pockets, throwing the dresses across their arms.

'The driver, the driver!' Tony hissed, pulling Harry back. The rain fell heavier, and they started to run. The driver spied the back of his lorry open and skittered forwards, but his heavy middle dragged him down. Loaded down with their contraband, the two made a break for it.

As they skidded around the corner of another alley, they tried not to plough into a shiny black Humber idling at the kerb. Its doors were open onto the pavement, the car weighed down, with skinny sleek-suited legs sticking out. Three guys – Hackers, Coshers, Harry would never remember – dribbled out of the car, their black coats hanging on their tall shoulders like pieces of the night. They surrounded Harry and Tony with a collective, predatory yowl, leering as the girls stumbled, laden with their stolen goods, out of breath in their shabby slacks and velvet pumps. *Evening,* one of them offered, pretending to be a gentleman. *A right couple of birds we have ourselves here*, another muttered, his comment greeted with a hush of obligatory laughs. The ringleader, Harry thought.

There was a loud *skat* on their left, and all heads swivelled. One King. Then two. Three, four, five, emerging from the other side of the street, coated, suited, booted. Kings. They fell around Harry and Tony like wolves protecting members of their pack, quickly outnumbering the guys. Tiffing, huffing, throwing their hands in the air, the boys smirked at each other. One of them wanted to speak, Harry could tell, chucking glances at each other, but no one managed it. All their words dried up at the flinch of Kings. Eventually, they shrugged it off with a *why-waste-our-time-on-this?* look and folded their long limbs back into the black car. These were the Kings, and the Kings were not to be messed with on this street. Or Edie would be after them, and no one wanted that. She was a handful. Bert, and the other Kings who were there – Lucia, Tweedy, Una, Pat – ushered them onwards into the night.

Harry and Tony, throwing back thanks, ran off into the endless rows of identical houses. Behind them, the Kings had started to mess with the lorry driver, goading him into thinking the girls had gone the other way. Harry caught Tony's eye and grinned, wildfire in them both, burning each other brighter. Tony hooted and smacked Harry's shoulder as they wheeled down the street, giddy, their bodies light as air. Patrolling coppers briefly lingered to consider if these kids were worth their time, but they let them scoot down the pavement. With their arms full, they were invincible. This cherry moment, running down the street with their new, ill-gotten gowns, was enough.

Emerging onto Wells Terrace, where they lived, Harry and Tony parted ways with a grin and ran into separate houses. Harry raced up to her family's flat, knowing her mother and sister were asleep, and found the loose floorboard inside the broom cupboard where she put her haul, alongside the notes and coins, scattered packets of cigarettes, ticket stubs. She thought her heart, beating fast, might roll out and clatter under the floorboards with her contraband. She dared not think *what now?* Edie would tell her tomorrow.

Then, she heard the shout: *Harry, Harry.* Not calm, not at all. Harry could draw the shape of her pulse from the noise of it. She tiptoed across the floorboards in the dark, cringing at the creaks. *Get down here!* The voice was unmistakeable: there, on Wells Terrace, was Edie.

She flew down the stairs and out into the street, without thinking. The rain had accelerated into a pour. Under its slick glisten, Edie twitched and fidgeted. Her cold hands grasped Harry's and she scrunched them with grappling affection. Her hair was wet and bedraggled, the sleeve of her blazer ripped. In the orange streetlight glow, Edie's jaw was blooming into a bruise.

'Come with me.' She tugged on Harry's arm.

'Is everything alright?' Harry asked, timid.

Edie pulled her through the close-packed streets, not responding, shivering, until they arrived at a bombsite – a scar, empty. Rubbish crunched under Harry's feet; junk surrounded them: parts of old cars and lorries, prams, bedsteads, spring mattresses with twisted wires, rusting gas stoves and dustbins, jagged tin cans. The rafters creaked and dripped. Edie heaved in and out as she crept under a makeshift roof of chipboard. She beckoned for Harry to join her.

'Edie?'

'I need you to do something for me, kid.' Edie's voice was steeled with a strange desperation. Was it the stolen dresses? Did she need to sell them on? Were the police after them? Would she have to give herself up?

'Anything.' The word was quick off Harry's tongue and she pressed herself under the shelter.

'I'm going away.' Edie darted her head around. 'I'm going away, tonight, and I need you to take over.' She looked at Harry, curiously. 'What do you know about how the Kings started?'

Harry recounted the story, familiar as the nativity, back at Edie as the rain fell about them: everyone said that Blondie Edie had been a stunner. A real looker. All the boys had wanted her, including the ones that already had girlfriends, who took slaps from those girlfriends just for the chance to look at her. Even the girls wanted her, if they didn't want to *be* her first. She pinched in her waist and stuck out her breasts; she spooled and piled her hair into the neatest page-boy styles; she wore skirts short enough to show most of her calves. It was her fault, the girls chorused. She was tempting them. Indeed, if something bad ever happened to Edie, then the general consensus was that it would have been her fault.

For as long as anyone remembered, Edie had stalked the streets around Finsbury Park, sipping a Coke on a squeaky-red stool at the bar while the boys made threats to each other over her; watching on from the sidelines – cheering, sometimes, if the mood was right – as the boys pummelled each other in the dirt. She was anyone's partner in the dance hall, anyone's date to the pictures, plushing out their nights, laughing at their jokes. Clutching the arm of whichever boy had the most power at the time. Just never at home, and never anyone questioning why. The jury was out on whether she even had one of those.

It all changed on one hot August night – so the story went. Harry had heard the tale so often that its many versions had begun to weave together into some monstrous plait, with details too specific to seem right, and timelines all whack and uneven. The story she liked the most went like this: while Edie sat around all those years at the bar, all innocent, all silent, she had been quietly amassing an audience of girls – the girls who hung around with her, on the edges of the gang, baubles for the boys. Legend had it that they hung on her words as she spoke and spun futures for them all. That hot August night, while the boys were brawling on a spit behind the church, kicking up dust from the dry scrubs of grass, she went to the Bridge, where the other girls – nearly ten of them – had agreed to meet. Slacked, skirted, blazered, hands in pockets. They walked across the Bridge and into new territory.

When the fight was over, the boys looked up and saw no one at their sidelines, no one cheering them on or ready to kiss their sweaty, dust-streaked faces. They howled through the streets, trying to find their girls – their *steadies* – but they were gone. Blondie Edie was no more. It was just Edie now.

The following night, Edie met them under the Bridge with a group of fifteen girls. The boys had only brought ten. To their surprise, Edie began to negotiate turf and territory. Rules, deals, bargains. She rattled off a list of which corners they shared and which they didn't, which shops were theirs to rob and which belonged to the boys. *You'll be so busy fighting with each other* – she had reassured them – *that you won't even notice us.*

Us? Harry could only assume the boys had replied.

The Kings, Edie had surely replied. *And in these streets, no matter what time of day, none of the Kings, not one of them, are to be touched.*

The boys had been stunned. But if the Kings were another gang, they argued, then they would have to fight like one.

'*Course*,' Edie taunted.

The girls arranged a brawl. The boys cancelled it. *We've got better things to do*, they said, never explaining what those better things were – other than hanging around the penny arcade and whistling at women from across the street. The Kings kept their territory. Then, the Kings expanded, picking up stray girls from the schoolyard. Harry had been one of them, kicking a football against the side of the cricket shed at the back of the school fields. She listened, mesmerized by Edie, always, the bounce of her hair, the swing of her hip as she walked. It was the first time Harry had lost her words, falling headlong into Edie's spell. After all, Edie had *chosen* her. *It's like an agreement,* Edie had said. *If one of us is in trouble, if she's out on the streets and needs help, she whistles. And if a King isn't there, then she will be soon.* Harry had said those words to Tony only a week or two later – and Tony had said them to another girl a week after that, while Harry watched on.

*

'That's not what happened,' Edie said, laughing. 'People like to think that I planned it all along, that I had it all mapped out. Or that, all of a sudden, Edie *flipped*. Makes a nice story, I s'pose.' She looked down, picking at her cuticles. Her blonde hair was black with the wet. 'No. What happened is that one of those boys wouldn't let me out of his sight that summer. I should have watched out for him, I should have watched *myself*, but he was smart. He waited until I was alone, behind the dance hall. I should have seen him coming.'

Harry hung on Edie's words like the raindrops on her lips.

'I'm not going to tell you what he did, if that's what you want,' Edie snapped. 'But I think you can imagine, anyway. He said he needed... he needed to be with a girl one last time before he went away.'

'Went where?'

'Army service. Conscription.'

'Who was it?'

'I'm not going to tell you that either. I don't want a bloody manhunt.' Harry felt her spine cool. She would never know if he had come back from the army. She would never know if it was *his* eye that lingered for a second too long on the street. 'But *that's* why,' Edie continued. 'The streets weren't mine anymore, and he made sure I remembered that they never had been. Something had to change. That's what happened.'

'Why didn't you tell anyone?'

Edie scoffed. She checked Harry, disbelief in her widening eyes.

'You think I'd want them all to know? To have them looking at me like some poor girl, some slut? And for the Kings just to be some kind of cheap *revenge*?' Her face cringed around the word. 'Just a chance to get back at the boys? No. No one can know about this.' Edie's eyes bored into her, her hair strange and rain-wild about her head. 'Not another soul.'

'Then, why *are* you telling me?' Harry was a little disappointed. She had already been imagining how she would serve this conversation up for the Kings tomorrow: *Edie was on the run, and she came to me.* And others would talk among themselves: *Did you hear how Edie came and found Harry, just before she went missing?* She had chosen Harry once at the cricket shed, and she had chosen her once again.

'Because you've got to understand, Harry, what this means. What the Kings mean. If I go away... when I go, because I don't think I'm coming back, then you need to be the one to carry this on, whatever it takes. You're smart, you can deal with this, I know you can. Someone invades the turf, you kick them out, beat them into the dust, what-ever you need to do. These streets belong to the Kings. All of these girls will rely on you, even if they don't know it.'

'The boys won't do us any harm, we're tough enough to take them on,' Harry vowed. 'I'd cut someone if he tried to hurt me.'

Edie smiled, wanly.

'That's what I always said, but it's hard to actually do it when his hand is on your neck.'

Harry stared at her.

'Is he back? Is that why you're leaving?'

'No. I've been caught.' As rain thwacked on broken surfaces around them, Edie explained that she was on the run from the police – she had bought some little white tablets from another gang and promised to sell them on, looking to grow into new business. But the man she sold them on to had been police. *How did you know?* Harry had asked. She knew. He told her. He tried to grab her, and told her that if she only kept quiet, and let him do what he wanted, then he wouldn't report her. She had shouted for the Kings. None came. He had kicked her into the gutter after she refused to let him take what he wanted. He would come back to her flat with a warrant for arrest. He had the evidence. He had her. She was done for. And even if he didn't come back tonight, he would come back soon enough.

THREE

1957

As Harry had predicted, the ringleaders of the Seven Sisters hated the proposition of the wager – but presented to them in the deserted park too close to closing time, in front of their Sisters and most of the Kings, where they would look foolish to refuse it, Sylvy and Char agreed and the match moved to a coin toss.

'Heads or tails?'

'Heads,' Harry replied. Char flipped the coin. Sylvy lingered on her right. Bated breath hooked the air. The Kings watched Harry's suit-back, gripped by the arrogant jut of her shoulder blades through the fabric, the bustle of curly-brown hair stiffened into submission by wax and a few dozen pins.

Char swore, sighed, looked off into the distance.

'Heads it is.'

'Heads it always is.'

Harry stalked back to join the line of six dark dots stretching across Finsbury Park. Concrete foundations from anti-aircraft guns and piles of discarded equipment dotted the brick-walled rolling grass, ruined from military exercises. It was no longer green, but a sea of mud with a few scrappy patches of tough grass poking up. A space for recreation, still, where the Kings met the Sisters every Sunday afternoon for a game of football. As was custom, they had marked out a makeshift pitch with a couple of suit jackets, and their core six played while ten-or-so others looked on. It was ritual; the Kings did not change. The Sunday football match did not change. They wore their Sunday suits right into the mud and would wear them six feet under.

The Kings scanned their opponents, seven of them lined up opposite like a wonky reflection. Sylvy, stationed in the centre, winked at stray boyfriends on the sidelines, loose Coshers smoking, chatting, slicking back their ducktails with small, discreet combs. She lit up under their looks, undistracted by Char tugging her sleeve. Sylvy's plain black suit was finely cut, and she wore a white shirt with ruffled collar spilling out over the lapels – well-layered and thoroughly, thoughtfully dressed. Her face, with its wide mouth clenched into a line, was hidden from the sky by an unkempt cloud of curly black hair. It was a shame, Harry thought, that she wore her heart on her sleeve despite all those layers of outward show. She wanted this turf, badly, and she couldn't help herself from doing whatever she could to get it.

'Spill, then. What's the plan?' Tony whispered, watching as Harry secreted a slim chiv in her tight cuff, patted her left breast to feel the reassuring shape of another blade in the inside pocket, and leaned down to itch her left ankle where a kukri knife hid in the sock. Harry was a walking weapon, a half-metallic slinger. 'Harry?'

'No plan. We play. We win.'

'I get that bit, but don't we want to—'

Harry told her to *shut it*. She stepped forward. The others followed.

The Seven Sisters mirrored their intimidation tactics – slow steps forward – until they stood almost chest to chest. Harry placed the ball on the floor, adjusting it once, twice, and then a third time in response to Char's huff on the second adjustment. She checked behind, looked at the faces of her Kings, and scanned her remotest peripheries.

She kicked the ball to Tony; the game was afoot. Tony hesitated for a minute, peppering it between her feet. Sylvy lurched forwards, as if to swipe it, leaving Tony to pass to Bert. Big-boned, big-headed Bert ran into the Sisters' half with no strategy. Bonbon (Bonnie to her parents), a slight thing with long legs, more fizz and energy than all the light bulbs in Islington, tackled the ball from Bert before running up the side of the pitch. Tony tackled the ball back from her, lunging in front. Harry voiced her support for Tony's move and gave coaching claps. She kept out of the action, choosing instead to hover like an umpire or a tiny god who had set a world spinning.

'Tony!' Leslie shouted, receiving the ball. Tony to Leslie to Jackie, the ball bounced easily and smoothly between the bodies on the green.

'Go for it!' Harry shouted, stepping in momentarily. Jackie did as Harry commanded, forgetting about her tightly permed hair and clean-cut suit to *thwack* the ball over the head of one of the Sisters. There was no net to hit the back of, but Jackie scored a goal anyway, sending the borrowed ball between two suit jackets. Unstoppable for the moment, she let her legs glide her around the pitch, punching the air as if to make a dent in it. The Kings hollered support, veering towards Jackie just to pat her on the back, enthuse themselves with her energy.

'Grow a few feet, and maybe you could save it,' Jackie mumbled while skipping back to the start line. Bonbon ran forwards and caught Jackie in a headlock; the two became pieces of a jigsaw puzzle stuck together incorrectly. Leslie ran to aid, kicking Bonbon in the shin, and Jackie managed to pull the arm away from her neck. From the other side of the pitch, Char shouted something over their heads that seemed to convey the message: *stand down*. Jackie smiled. The football matches were civil. The halfway scuffle gave way to peaceful play.

Tony moved to take the centre pass, and the other players mobilized into place. A small cloud slipped over the sun. Every now and then, Harry saw the cold glint of metal poking out from someone's sleeve or shoe or pocket.

The match continued with sticky, unfriendly passes. Midway through, as a vicious tackle was under way, a local policeman on his beat wandered by. He had shone a torch their way, even though it was still light out, and said *hey* and told them:

'Ten minutes until closing. You lot better not be here when I make my second round.'

His eyes lingered on the Coshers at the side of the makeshift pitch, his finger stubbing in their direction. None of them spoke in return or bothered to change their dead-set moony faces. There was no point, they knew, in engaging with the authorities. Their clothes and hair spelled menace. The article about their *ruckus*, *rampage* or *mayhem* had already been written, and when the newspaper photographers took their photo, the kids stared right into the soul of the lens.

Time spooled onwards, and, despite the evening's cold, the two gangs were sweating. The policeman would soon be returning. Weapons remained tucked up and sleeping under socks and sleeves. The Kings were on two goals to the Sisters' one; victory was near, their turf was near. The sky was turning royal blue – the tipping point of day. Civil twilight had long gone.

Saint, ever the stickler, yelled out *time*. She waved her arms frantically – *time, time* – while striding across the pitch.

'Time, that's it!' Harry scooped up the football and marched towards Char. 'That's it. The match is over. The turf is ours.' She placed the ball on the ground next to their feet.

Sylvy rushed in, panting at her, aflame. She put a hand on Char's shoulder and moved her aside, while a grin spilled across her face, panting.

'Don't you say it.' Harry shook her head. 'We had a *deal*.'

'Did we?'

'We won fair and square. It's ours and you know it.'

'No, I don't think so.' Sylvy picked up the ball and shoved it back into Harry's hands. The random Coshers – and the Sisters – skittered laughs into the night.

'No?' Harry locked her jaw. The other Kings folded in around and behind her, filings smothering their magnet. 'You're saying no?'

'Not a chance.' Sylvy smirked, eyes glowing. It seemed that even she was surprised, spurred on, by her own decision – and it was hers, and hers alone. A turn of events that she had created, the Coshers rumbling far behind, Char mumbling *don't Sylvy*. In reply to Harry's look, Sylvy asked: 'What? I don't know why you're so surprised about it. You weren't planning on giving us the territory either.'

Harry crossed her arms, shoved out a little scoffy laugh and, for better or worse, said:

'The thought of it never even crossed my mind.'

Dew sank on them in the stilling night, eyes flicking at each other.

Harry flipped out a blade, expecting to have a monopoly on the violence. But Sylvy was quick to react, unthinking, pressing a switchblade against an already existing scar on Harry's cheek. Harry kept a chiv pointing at Sylvy's abdomen. The Kings looked onto the sharp, bladed moment; the two girls, stubborn as hell, toe to toe.

'You should have thought about what would happen before you stole on our turf. But you don't think, do you?'

Sylvy pressed the blade down, making Harry lean her head back.

'I heard you got fired from the top job in the Sisters, Sylvy. For landing a punch on someone when you weren't supposed to, is that right? And that Char had to take over because you couldn't be trusted not to cause a fight.' This close, Harry could see the red welts on Sylvy's knuckles, the hard tortoiseshell brown of her eyes. No matter the situation, Sylvy could be counted on to answer back with violence. There was a chemical regularity to the way she tackled difficult situations, taking them down like bodies in her way. Like the newest, sleekest pistol, everyone knew that Sylvy would spit bullets.

'The turf's *ours*,' Sylvy said, simmering with fresh rage. She was about to blow, and Harry knew it.

Char puffed more *don't Sylvy*s from behind. *It's theirs, give it to them.*

'Are you going to cut me?' Harry goaded. 'Get it over with, in that case. Do you want a war, Sylvy? You'd better want one, because we won't let it go without a fight. You know that turf is ours, fair and square. You should listen to Charlie.'

'Don't call her that.'

A gate clanged.

'We need to go!' Saint shouted from behind.

A torch shined on their sweaty, muddy faces, momentarily lighting the glints of metal in their hands.

'Copper!' Saint yelled and began to tug on Harry's shoulder, dragging her off towards the darkness.

The policeman yelled uselessly at their retreating backs.

'We're coming to take it,' Harry said breathlessly at Sylvy as she retracted her knife and ran backwards to the edge of the bowling green. 'I'm not playing games, Sylvy.

I mean it.' Her eyes shone against the torch like a cat's, beelining for the edge of the lit patch as she climbed into the shadows with the rest of the Kings. Harry grabbed Tony's arm and dragged the drunk stumbler off the pitch. They disappeared into the night. Before the policeman could get close enough, the Seven Sisters also scattered with practised elegance and melted out of the torch beam. By now, the sun had sauntered far away, leaving the big, slabby sky squeaked clean.

The policeman made his way to the centre of the pitch. He saw nothing – perhaps his eyes were playing tricks on him again – and continued his closing-time inspection, before locking the gate for the night. The borrowed football had stilled on the pitch. One placeholding jacket remained, furling and unfurling in the evening breeze.

'Didn't I tell you—' Tony broke off, taking a swig mid-sentence. 'Didn't I tell you that this would end in a war?'

The table lurched into a murmuration of *too bloody rights*.

'Sylvy's pushed it too far,' Saint warned.

'And the others too,' the twins chimed, glooming at each other.

By now, The Kings Head was choke-thick with smoke – clogged with exhalation. The six Kings sprawled across the creaky wooden chairs, cluttered tables with their tosh, stickied the surfaces. Blaring orange lamps on the walls flamed the dried-blood red of the wood-panelled bar, the light pooling onto the paisley-patterned carpet. The streets were dead outside, but noise and nonsense burst from the Kings' corner, where the boredom of endless empty nights, dun silence, dull colour, had given way to this blown dam of conversation. They had claimed the pub – and by claiming it, had brought it to life, had made the colours run off the walls and the hours lose their pace. From the pub's snug corner, you could imagine yourself at the centre of the kingdom of Finsbury Park, roads spiralling outwards all the way north to the Woodbine Cigarettes Bridge and south to the end of Blackstock Road. The Kings Head, giving structure to the web of surrounding streets, was a holding cell for their future nights.

Even the Crone, who usually stood mindlessly polishing pint glasses behind the generous curve of the bar, had been shocked to life. The white-haired widow and owner of the pub floated around the tables, tending to solitary drinkers, chatting to the Kings in short spurts of affection. She didn't mind them; when the newspaperman had come to interview her about the *nuisance* and *blight* of youth on the streets and in the pubs, she had stared at him, perplexed. To make him leave, she said *you can't believe in all the press talk*, nodding towards his notebook; *it's all a build-up for the papers*. She hated the papers almost as much as she hated the police.

Edie had never admitted to the gang that she chose The Kings Head because of the Crone; she had never told the Kings that they would be hard-pressed to get service at any other pub (that the Kings knew), and the Kings never questioned it. This pub was theirs, through and through, by right and reason – theirs earned and won, forever.

Harry had not spoken for ten minutes. She sat in the corner, unsmiling, monarchically comfortable, keeping one ear open to the Kings' babblings and the other to the night. The Kings threw looks at her, waiting for a sign of movement as her eyes flicked around the interior, watching each worker after-hours, each chess player, each rogue teenager without a gang, wade through the thickening hours of their night. The only interaction that had taken place between the leader and any of the Kings was when Tony tapped a cigarette out of a packet and placed it on her ashy-red bottom lip, and Harry, watching her fish again in her pockets for matches or a lighter, stood up, struck a match, leaned over the beer-stained table and brought it to Tony. No thanks were given; none were needed.

Tony leaned back in the chair, almost useless for the night. The ever-present, now nearly empty hip flask lay side-down on the table. The twins had snuck away and were talking to a boy at the bar, who sipped his drink nervously and ran his hands through his greasy, shiny hair.

'I don't feel good about this, Harry...' Saint began, hushed, rubbing her fingers together. 'If we declare... a war, or whatever, power to the Kings and all that malarkey, what if we provoke the others, like the Hackers? We've always stayed afloat by not picking a fight, but what if we're sticking our necks out too much? Someone's bound to tell us to wind them in, or make us do it.' Saint paused, took out a piece of paper and looked at its scribbles. Harry saw the flicker of a smile shoot through her lips. 'If we go looking for trouble across the Bridge, how will we make sure we keep our turf *here*?'

Harry remained staring ahead, dragging on a cigarette.

'The Hackers are too busy fighting with each other to fight us,' Tony said. 'They know we're not looking to take them on.'

'But Marcus—'

'If Marcus wanted to take the turf, he would have done it by now. He knows us from school. About today, at the Dent: that was just for a laugh, you know?'

'Didn't look like you were laughing,' Saint muttered. Tony handed back a glare.

'Unless...' Saint continued. 'Unless we bring some more Kings on board.'

'What?'

'We can go to the schools this week. Most of the kids from Blackstock already know who we are, and we can give them corners to control.' Saint began scribbling notes, every now and then pulling away her pen hand to push her glasses up to the bridge of her nose. She shoved the pencil back behind her ear; a cigarette sat snug behind the other.

For the first time since entering the pub, Harry spoke.

'Tony, do me a favour, would you?'

'What's that?' She lifted her head off the table.

Harry took a drag. Then, polite as a button:

'For the past ten minutes, Sal has been stood outside. Tell her to come inside, will you?'

Sally – Sal when she was with the Sisters – leaned against the redbrick wall of The Kings Head. The galloping pace of her heartbeat lugged her back to the football match and the vision of Harry across the pitch, dart-eyed and glance-happy, dark hair piled ramshackle on her head. She had been glued to the skew of Harry's spine, Harry's left hand casually in her pocket, feet at right angles on the mud, the stub nose, almost chubby cheeks, the full moon of her face. Harry's lack of beauty never failed to surprise Sal, even as she became hypnotized near her. It was undeniable that the air shifted around Harry.

Sal was small, born unblessed in physical features. She was a latcher, a follower, the weakest link in the Sisters' chain. When she saw Harry on that pitch, she heard the chain snap. Sal's loyalty flipped on its head and she remembered the war and the train on which she and Harry had sat shoulder-to-shoulder with a hundred other kids who had never seen so much green; she remembered how they ended up in the same village, similar shithole farms, trudging through the same shit every day, counting the planes moaning across the wide summer sky. All Harry had to do was look at her and her allegiance began to shift.

The football match was Harry's gauge – that was obvious. A spirit level of the Sisters. It reminded Sal of the factory work that occupied her days: all pressure, gauges, forces, understanding how bodies of air react when they meet one another.

After the match, Sylvy came to her with a proposition. She had been home for only a minute when there was a knock on the door. Sal shouldered it open, dish in one hand, baby brother balanced on her love handle.

'Do me a favour, will you?' Sylvy had asked. She slipped a coin into Sal's hand and whispered a message into her ear in one slick movement, before patting her on the shoulder. 'Let me know what Harry says about *that*.' Thrusting her brother back inside, Sal pushed her way out of the flat and followed Sylvy's trace down the corridor.

Sal glanced her reflection in shop fronts as she walked to The Kings Head. She looked different, she thought: *purposeful*. Sal was reliable. You wanted her. She could do things for you.

Harry's words cut through the smoke like razorblades. The Kings twisted their necks and torsos towards the window, lifting their bottoms off seats, their eyes landing on a head of uncombed brown hair bobbing up and down outside the window; permed curls gathering the courage to sing. Tony clicked alert and pushed back her chair, lunging towards the door. Bert splayed her deck of cards slowly and neatly on the table.

After several moments, Tony re-emerged with Sal beside her. She looked to Harry for guidance. She studied the advertised quirk in her lip, the arched eyebrow, nothing quite in a straight line. The other drinkers ruffled in the background. The Crone turned her back on her best customers.

'Sal says she's brought us something,' Tony explained. 'Isn't that nice?'

'What's behind your back?' Bert stood, grabbing in her pockets for something defensive, more physical than words.

'It's nothing dangerous. Just a message.'

'From Char?'

'From Sylvy, isn't it?' Harry corrected Tony.

Sal nodded.

'Spit it out then.'

'If it's war that you want... then that's what you'll get. The turf belongs to the Seven Sisters and the Coshers now, and you'll have to kill the lot of them to get it back. You've no business even looking at our side of the Bridge. You've no business ever thinking about Seven Sisters Road. You can't win it by dancing the creep around us in circles and you can't win it with a football match either.'

'Keep going, take your time, Sal.' Harry sat back with a wide smile. She crossed her legs.

'Sylvy said that she would have discussed it, but now you can't even step foot past Woodbine Cigs Bridge or... we'll cut you.' Harry nodded, unshocked, absorbing the words. 'And Sylvy told me to give you this, as a gesture of... I don't really know, but something.' She drew out her hands, which held a football. Tony's missing football. The Kings waited for Harry to react.

After a considered pause, Harry laughed. The Kings looked at each other, confused enough to do nothing.

'I'm glad that Sylvy finds herself so funny,' Harry said, swiping an unseen tear from the corner of her eye with a pantomime finger-flick. 'Thanks for that. I needed a laugh after the past couple months.' She stood up, stubbed out her cigarette and stalked over to Sal, taking the ball out of her hand. 'Game on, then. If Sylvy wants to play, I'll play.'

She peppered the ball between her hands.

'Take a message back to Sylvy, will you? It's only short. But Saint could probably write it down for you, if you wanted.' Saint poised her pencil, then let it droop – unsure whether Harry was being serious.

'If *Sylvy* wants a war... she's got herself one. The next football match we play will be on her streets while the Sisters look on, while we steal from their shops and nick from their lorries and drink in their pubs. I don't want to scare you...' she gripped Sal's shoulder. 'It won't come to rough-and-tumble if it doesn't have to, you know what I'm like. Remember our time on the farms, eh? We know each other through and through.' Sal nodded, crumbling under the weight of Harry's full attention. 'If Sylvy wants to flaunt about it, then she's welcome to, but this is war. She's not safe this side of the Bridge, either. We're all Kings here.' She breathed deep, as if to finish. 'The Sisters are done for. You'd better understand that.'

Sal gave the least convincing nod of her life. Harry stepped around her and opened the door, gesturing politely for her to exit. She watched as Sal walked down the street, pausing to turn back every few steps until she disappeared under the Bridge.

When Harry returned inside, the Kings had bustled themselves into a roar, chanting *we're all Kings here, we're all Kings here*, smashing the fog-bent air into clarity, the voices falling over one another. As she sank back into her chair, she realized that one King was missing from the chorus. Harry's eyes swept over their corner of the pub, the empty hip flask tipped sideways on the table, dripping liquor onto the sticky wood. An old lipstick. A packet of matches. At the end of the trail, through a wall of drinkers, Tony smoked alone. She had smudged a porthole in the fogged-up window with her sleeve and looked out to another world. There was a time Harry would have gone over and talked to her.

The other girls danced into her vision, blocking Tony from view, and she couldn't help relishing that everything was on track. Sal's little visit was the final piece of the puzzle that she had planned in those celled moments alone. Harry had proposed the wager knowing, of course, that Sylvy would accept it in principle – and then refuse to grant her the territory. Sylvy would think herself smart, but Harry was four steps ahead. Harry had known that she would have to draw her blade, and that Sylvy would draw hers back, to incense the Kings. A cut meant war, and when Sylvy didn't cut her, Harry knew that she would need the last word: her declaration of war. They were all performing their lines to the letter, for the good of the Kings. Harry couldn't let them down. She couldn't let them die out like the piss-end of a candle.

The night was taut with plans.

FOUR

Nell was furious. Her close-cropped hair fell at angry angles across a blank forehead; her jawline was sharp. As she waited at the grammar school gates, watching the endless trudge-down of Islington's black-smudge roads, she stuck out her foot in little kicks, and pushed her hands into her pockets, as if looking for roots. She wouldn't drop her grudge. She wouldn't do it. She *refused* to – no matter what others expected of her. How could she move on so quickly, when her friend had stolen the kiss owed to her outside the council hall on Saturday night?

She replayed the night once more: how she'd stumbled out onto the fire escape, a rickety set of stairs around the back, and how she'd seen the mahogany-brown sheen of Drew's hair against a streetlight – with Petie's face locked onto his. Nell had been so shocked that she gasped hard on her cigarette and choked a lung's worth of air into the night. Still spluttering, she ran back into the pumping hall. She wondered if the knot of betrayal in her chest would ever loosen naturally: for all Nell's fiery popping, she hated confrontation and preferred living in the grudge, the half-boiled anger, feeling comfortable under the weight of a shoulder-chip.

'Afternoon,' Bernadette sang, emerging from the side street and jarring Nell. She was a deftly plaited little sprite, a wisp of body, her dull brown hair wound into intricate buds. Nell grumbled a greeting in reply. 'You're not *still* angry with Petie, are you?' Bernadette moaned. 'It's *Friday*.'

'Until she says sorry—'

Bernadette turned on her friend and began striding up the road away from the school. Nell rushed to catch up.

'It's not my fault!' She reached Bernadette, who pulled away again. 'Petie was the one who—' and again, Bernadette sped forwards. Nell jogged to keep up, panting. 'I was *promised* the kiss by—' Bernadette walking onwards, Nell running behind. The jagged push and pull continued. 'If you'll just listen to me!' Gaining enough ground to see the smile on Bernadette's face, Nell's lips also cracked into a smile of understanding. The push and pull evened out into a laughing tug. They were playing.

The two fourteen-year-olds slowed and began picking

their way across a patch of debris. They smiled at the two men clearing up the block and filling in the pocky bomb marks. These blights had been makeshift playgrounds for several years, but now they were undergoing a patching up. Every week, another smashed-up plot became of use to someone other than the children who spent hours reinventing worlds in them.

'What's this going to be, then?' Bernadette asked a construction worker with a brick in each hand.

'Until they can think of something better to do with it, it'll be a place to park cars, love.'

'You're just clearing the plot, not building anything new?' Nell checked. He shook his head. She sighed, her breath the colour of relief, and moved back to solid ground. She started muttering at Bernadette. 'Look, I'm just angry. I'd like to punch someone and if Petie's face happens to fall under my fist, then there's nothing either of us can do about it. It's just... *fate*, I s'pose.'

The road narrowed and the grammar school gathered at the dead end, retreating into itself and away from the main thoroughfare. Since passing the eleven-plus, Petie went to the state grammar school; Nell would remain at the comprehensive for another year, and Bernadette had dropped out of school altogether. According to her father, who worked in a haberdashery, she could add enough to sell ribbons and read enough to sell types of wool: *merino*, *angora, cashmere, mohair, virgin,* it was enough to earn a living. Bernadette, who always wanted to have a good time, claimed that it suited her fine. Living, earned or whatever, didn't sound too bad.

Petie's head breached the surface of a student ocean rolling towards the gates. The bright, blonde spark offset the oncoming greyness of the early winter afternoon. She strode towards them, jutting out her skinny legs.

Nell, with her right hand still shoved in her pocket, clenched the handle of the knife that she still couldn't quite believe she'd brought here. In an earlier haze of anger, bursting out the door, she turned back and grabbed it from the bottom drawer of her brother's bedside table. It felt stupid, now, thoughtless and heavy.

'Nell?' Petie questioned. In response, Nell stubbed the ground with a scuffed shoe. 'Still angry with me?'

'Fuming,' Bernadette said. 'Maybe smoke will start coming out of—'

'Shut it,' Nell snapped. She noticed the difference between their uniforms: her pinafore was rougher, shoddier, the contrast between her threadbare greys painful against Petie's crisp, logo-emblazoned blazer. Petie had ambition, *drive*, they said. She spoke so often of being a politician, a mayor, an MP, that Nell almost believed her – her glorious friend who had sketched out her future with the same precision as the pleats in her skirt.

'It didn't mean anything, Nell,' Petie said. 'When Drew leaned over to me on that dance floor with Elvis in the background, what did you want me to say? No?'

'Oh, shog off.'

'I can shog off? You came to my school gates.'

'I'm your friend, Pete!'

'Too right.'

'Then why kiss him?'

'There was nothing else to do. That dance was boring.'

'I could lay you out right here and—' She fumbled the blade out of her sleeve, realizing that the threat was nothing without it. A glint of late-afternoon sun crossed Petie's face.

'Nell!' Bernadette scolded.

'It's my big brother's.' Nell was unsure what to do with the thing. The weight felt awkward and ineffective. She was wielding a penknife, but she held it so dumbly, useless as a pencil.

Petie smiled.

'What now, Nell?' she asked. Briefly, Nell imagined slicing Petie into ribbons or jamming it into her theatrically, but both visions flew away quickly like unpegged circus tents. 'Are you going to cut me?' Petie asked again, crossing her arms. 'Go on, then.'

'I could…' Nell trailed off. The words, pre-rehearsed, dropped off her tongue. From around street corners, at opposite ends of bombsites and empty lots, behind park bushes, Nell had watched these scenes before – private performances of intimidation, of threats, of arguments and assault. In the Astoria, she watched boys on big buffy screens make ultimatums and flick out knives, scribbling down the movements, the words, the actions, on a mental tablet, repeating them to the night later in bed, as she tried not to hear the police sirens scrape the silence. She drew on this built stock of images in her head when wielding the knife, but her arm was at the wrong angle, her knife was too blunt and not the right kind, the words sounded different – hollowed out – when they came from her mouth. In her sister's clothes, with her brother's knife, Nell was barely Nell yet. Her performance was a cheap imitation.

'Cut it out!' Bernadette pushed her way between them and held up her hands flat-palmed to their chests. 'You so much as touch Petie with that blade and I'll cut you both up into little pieces. Cut it, not each other.' She paused, spilling over with a secret she wanted to share. 'Besides, the Kings will never let us in if we're squabbling like children.'

Petie halted.

'Kings? What about the Kings?'

'Tell her, Nell,' Bernadette directed, as Nell's blade began to droop. 'Tell her what happened yesterday.'

Nell lowered the blade to her waist, still gripping it tightly. Under Bernadette's stare, she folded it and slid it back into her sleeve.

'The Kings are recruiting,' Nell said. 'They came to me.'

'To *you*?' Petie crossed her arms.

'Let's not talk about it here,' Nell hushed them, glancing around. The trio began walking towards Blackstock Road, edging past the arcades on Seven Sisters Road, which were crammed to bursting, the duck-tailed dandies smoking on the pavements while their friends took turns on the machines inside. They passed under the Woodbine Cigarettes Bridge, plunging deeper into the maze of terraced roads off Finsbury Park. The houses gathered closer together with every street, as if for warmth, penguin-blocks of flats and cramped terraces vying for the heat swirling about in the air.

'Tell me.' Petie swatted her impatiently.

Nell smirked, holding on to the information – *her* information – for a moment more. Petie rolled her eyes at the theatrics.

'Joan – Saint, that's what all of them call her' – Nell savoured the nickname, reserved only for friends. '*Saint* came to the school gates on Tuesday. Asked me if I wanted to earn some pennies, have some fun and cause some trouble.' The meeting still glimmered in Nell's memory, gold-plated, hallowed. She had been kicking a football against a brick wall when three taller figures had approached like silhouettes cut loose from paper. Nell knew who they were: the Kings. Petie went on and on about how she lived next to Tony and how she loaned the Kings footballs sometimes when Tony inevitably lost them. She claimed their shared wall as a connection of some higher sort; that they were, on some ideological or intellectual level, *kin*. Yet the Kings had come to Nell.

Saint had introduced herself, complimented Nell's hair. *You're bored, aren't you?* Saint had asked. Nell could only agree. What, Nell had thought, would she tell Petie? *You want to ride with us?* she asked. Nell could only nod. Saint had started talking then, without questions and without the gaps for Nell to ask them. Speaking in lengthy circles, she sold – seemingly for free – a vision of endless streets paved with their names, theirs forever. Nell knew there was a cost to it all; she just hadn't figured it out yet.

'There's a war,' Nell relayed. 'The Kings and the ones across the Bridge, the um… the Sisters. We could help, Saint said.'

'The Seven Sisters,' Petie corrected.

'We're going to say yes, aren't we?' Nell asked, pulling the two of them aside. Petie chewed on her lips and looked at the slat of sky between the roofs. 'We have to, Pete. We could go around with them, it would be the dream. We'd be untouchable.'

'I want to dance in a dance hall and drink in the cafés late at night.' Bernadette grinned. 'With the Kings, we can do that.'

'C'mon, *Petunia*.' Nell elbowed Petie, using her full name to rankle her.

After a long time, Petie nodded.

'That settles it, then,' Bernadette chirped, hands on hips. 'You two have got to make up. It's completely... unprofessional. If we go to see the Kings while we're having our own tiffs, they'll turn us away. Now, shake hands.' Bernadette's voice was flat and hard. Petie held out a hand. Nell reached out to take it. As their fingertips touched, a kid pushed through them, running full pelt.

'Sorry,' the voice piped up, breathless. Bernadette caught the sleeve of his jacket before he could run any further. 'Hey, I'm running for a doctor,' he protested. With the determination and importance of having been given a *task*, he twisted, tried to tear away from Bernadette, who held on tightly to his sleeve. Her features softened in concern.

'Who's hurt?'

'Not hurt, *dying*.'

'Who?' Petie shook them.

'Mr George,' the kid mumbled. Bernadette let go. The kid scrammed.

'I never thought Mr George would be able to die...' Bernadette said. 'He would get close, but each time, when he got close, he'd come back.'

'But he won't be *gone* though, really, will he?' Nell said.

Mr George had been stuck to the street longer than anyone. Longer even than the lamp-posts, Nell thought. Laughter and heavy time crinkled his face. He carried acres, canons, traditions in him. A legend of sorts, his head stocked with endless shelves of anecdotes and memories that everyone quoted back at him. And he spoke to them in a language sprinkled with *m'dears* and *darlings* and *loves*. Mr George had lived through both wars, fighting on the battlefields in one and on the streets of London in the other. The war might be over, the streets changing shape, but Mr George was constant, inevitable.

'Remember when Mr George asked me to tie his shoe-laces last week?' Petie laughed. 'He's got so fat that he can't reach his feet anymore and he grabbed the back of my shirt and gave me a liquorice and told me to tie them and shut up about it.'

'Remember,' Bernadette stuttered, 'when Mr George would tell us about what it was like in Victoria's time with corsets and carriages and big floofey dresses...'

'Or when he told us about the war... how he was in the Home Guard with your uncle, Petie, and they'd walk around at night knocking on people's doors if they could see light under the blinds.'

'Or when Mr George told us about Harry,' Petie added. 'How Harry had helped save him from giving up his flat when his wife died and he couldn't work anymore.'

70

The trio walked on, their tales of Mr George fading to silence. Trying to lift the new weight that had fallen between them, Nell launched back into discussion of the Kings. The stolen kiss, forgotten in this mash of reminiscence and excitement, was left in the dirt somewhere outside the school gates.

FIVE

No one was really watching the film playing in the cinema. They were all too nervous about what would happen. Not in the film – the Kings had all seen this one before. And besides, it was obvious: the blonde girlfriend would give away the gramophone full of stolen diamonds (because apparently that's where crooks hid their diamonds) to the policeman's son, and the policeman's son (because he was a policeman's son) would want to hand the diamonds in to the police. After some chase, the crook would be caught, the diamonds returned, and the credits would roll. In fact, the film's confidence in its own logic was a comfort to the Kings, from the girlfriend's easy silence to the fake gun cracks. Its uninteresting, predictable bulk was a ground they could pitch their tent on. No, the film was fine. Their nerves were mostly to do with the rest of the night that lay ahead. No blondes, no gramophones, no diamonds. Just Harry, seething in the back row of a dank, dark cinema.

Harry felt their jitteriness leaking towards where she sat by the aisle. The twins tattling, trying to stopper their nerves with all the words in their mouths, while Tony, feet on the seat in front, flicked her way noisily through a magazine, reading out the horoscopes. Saint picked the cuticles from her nails, rolling them up into little balls of dead skin and dropping them to the floor. Perhaps it was for the best that they were all wrapped up in their own distractions; it would be harder for them to notice Harry's shaking hands.

Stuffing them in her pockets, she tried to pinpoint the moment when her hands had begun to shake, to root out the problem like a bad tooth. She was quite sure it had something to do with the kids she'd found on her doorstep earlier that day, one of whom was Petie MacDowell, her little tears dripping onto the bricks.

Harry, Petie had breathed, shooting up like spring. She brushed the tears from her eyes in stealthy swipes.

What are you lot then, pigeons? The phrase came quickly to Harry – and it was better than nothing. Act further ahead than you are, she'd learned from Edie; the mind would catch up in time.

Harry, I'm really sorry. Petie looked at the ground.

What's happened? Harry might have grabbed Petie's shoulders, but she couldn't remember much. After Petie said *Mr George is dead*, her head stopped storing

73

memories, her eyes and ears suddenly fuzzed up with blur. The three kids were chattering about how Mr George had been *calling out* and *mumbling all kinds of things* before his *heart just stopped*, and a wave of dull ache was turning over in Harry's stomach. Those were too-familiar feelings in a too-familiar place.

Nearly a decade before, Harry's mother had sat with her on their doorstep and said *your father's dead* and Harry had done her best to feel nothing, even when Mr George found her sitting there still, hours later, and told her to feel something, especially the pain, or she would risk feeling nothing ever again. If someone deserved to be remembered forever, she had thought then, it was Mr George, with his round belly and his laugh like a Christmas cracker. *You can't keep torturing your mother like this*, he had shouted at her when the late nights and split lips became too frequent, when she forgot to be careful. During their fights, they looked funny – her slight frame set in opposition to his bulk, yelling at each other in the gloom, her voice harder than his soft reasonings. People said that he went quiet after she got sent to Holloway. *Strange.* Since she'd been back, she had meant to knock on his door and apologize to him, talk to him, tell him he was right, ask him whether he understood. All week, she had been nurturing the courage, and now it was too late.

In front of Petie and her friends, the dull grief had threatened to sharpen and she stepped backwards from the house. Petie had asked *didn't she want to go inside? Didn't she want to see him one last time?* but, still reeling, Harry had replied by demanding whether the three girls had made up their minds about joining the Kings. One of the kids shot up and shouted *yes!* and Petie had nudged her, dampening her friend's enthusiasm for fear it would make them seem childish. Harry had assured them there was plenty of space for three more Kings, or there would be very soon. *Welcome to the Kings*, she had told them. The girls had grinned at each other, shining and sincere.

She stepped further and further back into the street; a car blared its horn and she shoved up two shaking fingers at the driver. Someone swore back. From across the road, she shouted at Petie: *If anyone asks, I wasn't here*. Petie asked why she was leaving. *There's somewhere I need to be*, Harry replied. *Something I need to do.*

'Are you sure it was a good idea to ask her to come here?' The question – whispered from Saint beside her – drew Harry back to the cinema. On the screen, the crook was showing his girlfriend the kitchen in their new house. He grants her permission to caress the kitchen cupboards and she strokes them like a horse's flank, with wonder. He allows her to marvel at the stream from the taps. *All mine?* she asks, delighted. 'What if she comes in here looking for a fight?' Saint continued, her warm, jeaned thigh touching Harry's.

'She wouldn't,' Tony said, on Saint's right.

'But I'm just saying what if she does?' Saint pressed.

'Then, that's why we're at Roddy's, I s'pose. It's empty this late, no witnesses. And not exactly anywhere for her to... you know, *run*.'

'Witnesses to what, Harry?' Saint asked, wide-eyed. No reply, as usual.

Roddy's Rink – of questionable reputation – stood in the shadow of the Bridge, cupping the edge of Blackstock Road and almost within eyesight of The Kings Head, sandwiched between the two territories. It was new, comparatively speaking, and attracted locals like a honey trap, with its sweet grease smell slipping through the air, the rattle of oiled popcorn kernels turning over in the lobby. People said the cinema would last another few months, if Roddy was lucky. He was the previous owner of Roddy's Arcade and Roddy's Club, and this was the latest in his line of precarious investments – precarious because he invested so little. Paint dwindled newly, the brushstrokes too visible. And anyone who was anyone knew that the corners were painted black, the seats reclined and the loud pictures – louder than most other cinemas – kept rolling one after the other. Women were had, for fees. Men made deals at the back door. Trades carried out, in secret, cash sifting through hands like sand. No one was watching too closely at Roddy's.

Roddy himself would soon be here to lock up; this was the final flick of the night. The Kings had already been here for hours. Roddy never minded them, or how long they stayed.

'Are you alright, Harry? You're awful quiet,' Jackie asked from further down the row, leaning forwards. Leslie shushed her twin.

Harry nodded. She would be alright after she had done what she needed to do – to make sure the Kings lived forever, to solidify their reign, to exert power. She would be alright in a few short moments. For now:

'Is she here yet?' Harry craned her neck around. As if on cue, the doors burst open, and Bert strode in.

Bert would go to the grave swearing that she'd never meant for it to happen. She was Bert, Harry's Bert, *loyal* Bert, who had stuck with Harry through thick, thin, and thick again; a King through and through, whether you tested her blood, water, sweat or sighs, it came out King. When her family's home was an ashy pit after the war, she had lived with Harry – before the state sent them to different countrysides. They had lain awake in Harry's single bed, their mothers crying in the kitchen. Across the pillow, Harry had saturated her with vision. The pitch of golden promises had slipped into Bert's head and she had bought into Edie's gang hand and foot, heart and soul. She went from *dear Roberta*, with her bulky frame and bullish nose, her hair wilder and taller than the others, to *Bert? Harry's Bert? You'd better watch out for her.*

She would swear that it wasn't her fault, that she had to find escapes from her husband every now and then. The Kings never understood why she *had* a husband, what she needed him for, but marriage had been easy to romanticize at eighteen, when it was all schoolyard romance, big talk and a small gold band. Bert had told him that it was an agreement, and he was on her page. She would wait for him to complete his military service, and when he returned they would have some fun, save up some money, laugh about life together. When the time came, she supposed, there would be children.

After her husband returned home, he was scattered. He broke too many things at the factory, and shouted too often at the men who were above him. Bert's job only paid half of his in the first place, so when he was let go, she turned to the Kings and Harry's promises to fill her pockets with spare change. But while she told herself it was just about the cash, the buzz and the unpredictability of the Kings filled her up like nothing else, shining through the routine of domestic life. Kicking someone in the face, kicking a football, kicking around ash with her Kings, kept her from thinking too hard about her own reality, for now.

Every day, when the washing-up was done and the laundry had been folded and the papers had been read and Bert's husband stared at the wall saying nothing, and she could say nothing to him, the long evening hours stretched empty in front of them, suffocating. He barely noticed when she left their two-room flat and plunged into the night.

You couldn't blame her for preferring the arcades on the wrong side of the Bridge, where she could slip from her role as wife and homemaker into carefree anonymity. She was always sure to keep her eyes to herself and not stick her neck out, but their canteens and pin-table bars had better music, the Coke was colder, and the windows rarely got fogged up. Besides, if she were to overhear the Sisters discussing their next move, or spy on the Hackers discussing which gang to fight, the information would make her invaluable to Harry. The Kings had recently grown a terrible habit of not listening to her. *Mrs Dean*, they sometimes called her, voices dripping mockery.

Becoming Sylvy's spy was the last thing Bert expected. Several weeks ago, as Harry was still languishing behind the prison walls, she had lingered too long near the Bridge. Noises, figures – but only Sisters, much to her relief – ambushed her in the shaded stretch below the stars. After exchanges of *oi* and *bugger off*, where the Sisters shunted Bert against the wall, Sylvy had joined and a meeting of sorts was soon under way, without anyone intending for it to happen. Partly out of gratitude that the Sisters weren't going to shiv her, Bert lost sight of her promise to Harry when Sylvy offered her some banknotes in exchange for information. She could still remember how the streetlights turned the paper orange, pushing the darkness off. A loud buzz droned in the background, with the lamps changed from gas to electric that summer; a collection of bees tasked to annoy, confuse and upset. Brutal amber bulbs replaced the four-walled gaslamps that had shed soft, pale-yellow waves.

At Sylvy's invitation, Bert returned the following night. They waited for her in one of their bars. Bought her a drink. Sat her down and thanked her for coming. No one had ever thanked Bert for coming anywhere before. She told them about the turf near the Bridge and at what times the Kings stopped watching the corners; which shops Harry cared about, and which she didn't. Weeks passed, and when Sylvy took the turf Bert had no qualms. She was their informant; their go-to girl. She told herself it was all worth it because she had a new set of dishes stowed away in her kitchen cabinets, a new suit, and money to pay for her husband's psychotherapist appointments that were a secret from the rest of the family. She cultivated a routine, sitting in the corner of The Kings Head, absorbing the gusts of rumour and plans that blew from Harry, Tony and Saint. Afterwards, she sidled to the edge of the Bridge, where shadow becomes moonlight, to relay the news to the girls who were waiting for her.

Bert would never even have considered betraying Harry. None of what she'd done was grand enough for the word *betrayal*. These were desperate times, and she had needed desperate, indiscriminate measures. It was all really quite necessary, she reasoned.

Chomping at her nails outside Roddy's, Bert had a terrible feeling that she was not here to see the film. But Harry couldn't know, could she? She never paid any attention to Bert. They made it clear that, as a married woman, Bert had somehow already betrayed them. She had been so careful not to sit at window-tables with the Sisters, not to be followed from The Kings Head. Every night this week, when she had retreated from their territory and crossed the invisible divide into the other, she had listened for footsteps and heard none. Harry wouldn't know unless someone had told her.

Bert stretched out the final embers of her cigarette, watching the ash crumble and fall lazily. Huffing, she threw it to the ground, mashing it into the pavement as if trying to make a mark. She fingered her back pocket and the gentle ridge protruding through the woollen suit trousers. The switchblade was just for precautions, she told herself. Harry was her oldest friend, and she had nothing to worry about.

Cigarette stubbed, she searched for reasons to stay there a little longer. But the night was running on its clock. She pressed into the building with the energy of a wasting tornado.

On screen, as she entered, a boy was hanging onto a tower with one hand, gramophone in the other, his fingers slipping off the metal bar one by one. Bert paused on the lip of the room, waiting for the fall.

'Psst!' The sharp hiss rocked her attention. It was Harry, beckoning her over to the back row clogged with Kings. Bert forced her legs to move forwards, briefly looking again at the screen – but it had cut away to a kitchen table, water boiling in a saucepan, a phone ringing. Mundane stuff. Who knew if the boy was dead, falling through the seams between the scenes into some strange eternity.

'Alright?' Harry asked, a forced brightness in her eyes. She leapt out of the seat and embraced Bert in a loose hug. Two taps on her back. Bert couldn't remember Harry being so thin before she went away, or her eyes so sunken, or her hands so shaky.

'The kid's fine, don't worry,' she said, noticing Bert's glances at the screen. 'Turns out he's hanging onto the ledge.' Bert felt this reassured her more than it should have. She smiled, greeted the other Kings, who were slapping words around to each other, casually lolling in their seats.

'Come on, then, take a pew. Sit next to me. Go on, Saint, move up. There we are.' Harry herded them like chickens. Before Bert could protest – not, of course, that she wanted to – she was wedged into the seat between Harry and Saint, both of whom put their feet up, fencing Bert into a sort of pen. Not a lot of room to breathe, or escape.

Harry flipped open a pack of cigarettes and offered them around. Polite *no thank you*s left her arm suspended. She rushed on.

'So, have you heard about how many kids we've convinced to join us on this barmy ride?'

A nervous silence fell around them, the film droning on.

'Well?'

Urged *how many*s and *tell us, then* responded in a panic.

'Funnily enough, I've lost count, now that you ask. But three more this afternoon. Plenty of Kings now. Maybe *too* many.' The way Harry fixed her eyes on the screen as she spoke was unnerving. Not that looking into them ever gave anyone an edge on what she was thinking.

'You can never have too many Kings, Harry,' Bert said, twisting in her seat to get a look around. She counted five other heads in the room – two of which seemed to be occupying the same seat.

'What are you squirming for?' Saint asked. She was clacking a lollipop around her teeth.

'Wondering if the bar's still open,' Bert replied. The ease of the lie was surprising. Saint quickly informed her that it was closed and the show was nearly finished anyway, so they could find a drink afterwards. It was a perfectly reasonable explanation to keep Bert from getting out of her seat.

'Do you remember that kid yesterday?' Harry mused in Tony's direction, turning away from the screen. She wavered, but, catching Harry's eye, started to nod.

'Sure, what about them, Harry?'

'I was having some trouble making up my mind about what to do with them. Maybe you could help,' she said, gesturing at Bert.

'What did they do?'

'She was old enough to know better, about sixteen, I reckon—'

'Seventeen,' Tony interjected.

'Thanks, Tone, *seventeen*. She must have been drunk, but she came into the Head, barely hanging onto her wits. She came stumbling up to me and started hitting me, not that hard, just enough to make a scene.' In an attempt to re-enact the encounter, her fists were stage-fighting an invisible chest in front of her. 'And she continues to hit, smack, tries to scratch my cheek, look here... and then she starts mumbling this load of rubbish about going over to the Seven Sisters because I'm crazy and off my rocker and who do I think I am?' She paused, breathless. 'So, what did we do, Tone?'

'We, uh...'

'That's right, slap her up a bit and throw her out in the hopes that the night might swallow her whole.'

'We... let her go.' Tony tripped over the silence.

'Exack-ly. But you see my problem here, Bert?'

Bert shook her head.

'The problem is that I'm lying in bed last night and all I can hear are this kid's words in my head. I can smell her breath on my skin and I'm in a real mood with my two-hours-ago self that made that stupid decision to let her off. Because I wish I'd gutted the fool. I really do. But it's too bloody late, because I can't get my hands dirty right now. You know that, don't you? With all this war over the streets hanging in the balance, I've got to keep my hands tidy, you understand?'

'What do you want *me* to do, then? Cut them?' Bert guessed, hushing her voice from the Kings, who were laughing at something happening on screen. 'What do you want me to say, Harry?' Harry turned back to the film, shrugging.

'I just want your advice. You always give good advice, ever since we lived together in the war. Think of those nights.' Bert did. 'What do you say? If you had some troublemaker like that come up to you in front of a pub full of people and threaten to betray you, what would you do? Could you have slept, knowing the bastard was walking the streets?'

A man staggered up the aisle, a cloud of alcohol on his heels. Bert looked at him longingly, and found herself wondering who was waiting for him at home. She should enjoy this, Bert told herself, hanging with the Kings, with Harry, like old times – but the buzz had spilled over into the achy tinnitus that comes after the beautiful racket.

'No,' Bert replied, eventually, still tracking him as he left. She repeated it, directly to Harry. 'No, they've got no right saying that about you. You need… to cut her. What if she starts spewing stuff like that to her friends?' Bert whispered over the pricked hair of Harry's ear, just as they had done on that springy mattress looking up at the hole in the roof. 'All you need to do is find a dance hall that plays the music so loud you can't hear the screams. You need to go up to her in the middle of a song and shiv her.' Harry pulled back slightly. 'That's how the boys do it... that's how we do it in Finsbury Park.'

'You're too paranoid.' Harry laughed it off.

'I just *care*.' Bert smiled in return.

'Even though she didn't actually turn traitor, just threatened to, you think that was enough for a cutting?'

Bert nodded without a single pulse of hesitation. Her mind was tuned to yes – say yes to everything Harry asked. And Harry seemed satisfied with the answer. She moved on.

'Look, we haven't got all day. Let's get to the real order of business, shall we? Saint?'

Saint crunched down hard on the lollipop, startling Bert. She pulled out the clean, white stick, sucking it clean. With a rare smile, she drew a roll of paper from behind her ear that could have passed for a cigarette. She scanned the scribbled pencil notes, then looked up and glanced at Harry. Harry glanced at Tony.

'Business?' Bert muttered. 'I thought we came to Roddy's to hang about.'

'We want to get rid of the Kings who grassed us up.' Bert inched forwards in her seat. The music heightened for the film's final moment as the girlfriend, face glistening with tears, had nothing to say. Not a peep, not a protest. 'The Kings who grassed us up. That was you,' Saint clarified, casually.

Bert slinked further forwards. The film was over, the credits about to roll, so why was everyone shuffling to the edge of their seats? Everyone but Harry. She remained still.

'Say that was the case... you – you know about my husband,' Bert spluttered. 'I needed a few bob, and Sylvy threatened me, and – and, I wasn't in a position to turn her down, I swear, I had no choice—'

'One minute ago, you were quick to cut someone for threatening to betray, and now, when you're on the gallows, you say cut the noose, let you off the hook?'

A few more looks left, right. Left, right. Then Bert tore out of her seat, launching herself over the row in front. Harry grasped at the tail of her jacket, but she was too fast, hurdling the rows one by one towards the screen, as if she wanted to climb inside it, wrap the silver around her like a dressing gown. The Kings pursued, scaling the rows to reach her, some steaming down the aisle to try to catch her before she made her getaway. The credits were rolling, a rock 'n' roll tune cranking out over the speakers. Something about *doing anything for you*.

'Look, I admitted it, alright?' Bert shouted backwards as she clambered over seats. Protests from a woman who appeared to have been sleeping, as Bert caught her foot in the loop of the woman's handbag. 'Doesn't that mean something?' she huffed. Harry pursued. 'Don't be using big words like *traitor*.'

'If it was money that you wanted, Bert, why not come to me? Why not steal it on your own terms? You could have asked me, but instead you go to *them*—'

'They came to me—'

'—and you sell me out for a couple of quid.'

The chase paused, Harry stood at one end of a row, Bert at the other, slightly precarious with the cushioned velvet under their feet.

'I didn't think I'd be worth so little to you, Bert.' Harry stepped one seat closer. Bert stepped one back, as if that cancelled it out. She flicked the switchblade out of her pocket. Kings froze around her. Bert wouldn't have believed she was holding it – and at Harry nonetheless – if she hadn't looked right and seen their silhouettes shone onto the screen. The projector light screamed on their left. The flicks never did stop rolling at Roddy's. Harry continued:

'I thought you would say no, thank you, *Harry is my friend and a King and believe me, I wish I could, I really do, but I have to go now.* But you counted the money out and put it in your pocket and now look where we are.' She gestured around her: surrounded by Kings, a blade in Bert's hand, the floor laced with menace.

'You can't betray something if it's nothing.'

'The Kings aren't nothing.' Harry moved another seat further forwards. 'All this *few bob* excuse, everything you're saying, it's all a load of old cobblers, Bert, and you know it.'

'The Kings are *nothing* and you know it.' Bert – as much as she tried to stop it – felt the sting of tears.

'Well, the Kings *will* be nothing with kids like you, Bert. We have to stick together, not go turning traitor. That's how we stay on top.' *That's how we stay safe.* Unsaid on Harry's tongue.

'I'm not a kid.'

'And you're not a King, either.' Harry waved her hand at Bert. 'I thought I had a real uprising on my hands, but it was just a greedy girl looking for another penny to spend on her fucking hair. If that's what you want to tell yourself.'

'You can't throw me out, I don't know what I'll do without—'

'You should have thought of that before.' Harry charged, and Bert turned and ran. She leapt across the aisle, but it was wider than expected. Her leading ankle, caught in an armrest, twisted in the opposite direction from her body. She heard it *crack*. Pain rushed in and she crumpled to the floor, the room's heavy velvet furnishings muffling her yell of agony. Then, the room stilled, the sound of their skirmish all eaten up.

Harry leisurely walked to the end of the row, and stood on the aisle seat. She bore down on Bert, a look of roiling anger that she had not been able to fix things – for herself, for Bert.

Tony appeared beside her, standing on the aisle seat of the row in front.

'As Harry has made it clear, Bert, you're out,' she explained. Her voice was harsh at first, but it softened. 'That means no stepping foot in The Kings Head. No selling, dealing, stealing or trading – no partaking in any operation of any sort whatsoever – in Kings' territory, which, very soon, might include both sides of the Bridge.'

'Who says you can just decide that?' Bert's voice groped at the air, grovelly, stone-thick. 'We're all Kings here, remember?'

'We're not all Kings here, not anymore,' Tony whispered.

'Get out!' Harry shouted. 'The Kings don't want you. You sold us out. You could've brought down this whole territory and you could have put everything at risk.' She paused, sneering. 'Go back to *your man*. Maybe he'll keep you safe.'

Bert dragged herself up the aisle and towards the door, her leg trailing loosely behind. She looked back, sadly, before the building vomited her back into the cold, lonely night.

Slumping down into the seat, exhaustion written all over her, Harry lowered her head into shaking hands. It was a strange sight: the Kings had rarely seen her so affected.

The silence was thick between them, the film reeled through. Someone snapped off the projector.

'The coppers will call this one of them riots,' Tony tried to chuckle as the final couple rushed out, mumbling something about reporting the *disturbance* to the police.

'Sounds about right,' Saint replied. Cinema riots were springing up all over the country like shoots of water from concrete, the music too much for the kids to stay in their seats.

'That settles it,' Harry said, after a while. She smiled tightly, waiting for the unfinished feeling to pass. A trailing sense of doubt huffed through the air. She knew the scene had been too much, but she'd had to be sure that the night would leave a mark on the Kings: *her* Kings. They would remember the chase and the film and the shouting and the *crack*. No King would turn traitor again.

'That settles it,' she said again, and got up to leave, the Kings following close behind.

SIX

Cecil's favourite attraction in the arcade had always been the Grip-Teze. Costing only a penny and paying out pleasure upon pleasure, the slot machine awarded strength by stripping the clothes off a little figure inside a peephole. He grabbed the handle with both hands, gritted his teeth, and stared as shoes, skirt and blouse layered off and a bikinied body shone into the apple of his eye. A bell dinged and the rating swung to *oh boy!* as young men jeered around him. Someone passed him a cigarette, which he sucked dry and handed back, a wide grin on his face.

Give it another go, then, they slapped Cecil's back and thrust pennies at him, crowding around his shoulders. Was he supposed to keep gripping and stripping, round after round? How many pennies had he fed into this machine and what had it offered him in return? He was no more satisfied than when he stepped into the arcade an hour ago. Not to mention that his arms were killing him, his muscles sore and screaming. Calling himself a fool for thinking too deeply about it, he once again gripped and waited for the rating – *oh boy!* – which he knew would come (often regardless of how hard the player gripped the handle) and stepped back for the others to look at this nearly-naked woman in the peephole.

Around him, the arcade dazzled with pinging lights; it was a kaleidoscope of play. Late on Friday afternoon, every kid with a coin and teenager with a spare hour was here. A prolonged, grey drizzle had clenched Seven Sisters Road outside the glass front, giving the interior a sticky, humid frenzy. The twanging coins and flipping switches, the dinging, clinking and jingling, and the rattling shots from the firing range upstairs crammed Cecil's senses like cotton wool. The busy walls were splattered with tattoo designs, Coca-Cola adverts, posters for competing films – a boxy, purple-orange one for *Violent Playground* at the Odeon Astoria across the road, with a hooligan thrusting a tommy gun at a classroom full of children; and a yellow-red-blue one for some crime melodrama at Roddy's Rink, featuring a close-up of the beautiful Belinda Lee. One of the young men who worked with Cecil at the garage, grease still behind his ears, had tried and failed to recreate her facial expression, something between longing and flirtation, groaning in desire, but it fell flat and they were all a bit embarrassed for him, though none would admit it.

The puppet Sidney Knows watched Cecil from the corner. Let loose from his strings to career in a glass box, Sidney encouraged players to give a penny and receive a future career card. For this small fee, the player could buy happiness in the shape of a desk and a salary. Red clumps of hair stuck to the doll's head, glazes of glue showing on the scalp. Cecil drew closer to Sidney, his hand hovering over the coin-eater, which read *Slide In*. Shouts from behind lurched in his chest and he snapped back to the others, gripped by the dread that someone might see him with a hand near a girl's game. He wouldn't live that down for weeks.

High-pitched laughs rolled into the arcade with the opening of the door and he turned his head, ready to seduce, before his brain caught up with his eyes. He cringed upon seeing his older sister Sylvy – with her gang. Glorified girlfriends, he smirked. Cecil felt safe knowing that others ridiculed her too, with her ruffled shirts, black suits and pinned-up hair, looking nothing how a girl should look; the silk scarves and glitzy brooches that were far more expensive, even at the reduced prices, than she could actually afford. All of her tough talk and tough walks, strutting through the streets that she thought she *owned*. Cecil scoffed. It was pure fantasy. When the Coshers came back from overseas and the tail end of female independence dried up, then he'd like to see her put on all that gaff and call the streets her own.

He knew that she stole most of it – the clothes, the money, the cigarettes. She had always been quick with her hands, where Cecil's were quivering and skittish, much like the rest of his body. He was thin as a sapling and the worst kind of tall, like stretched taffy, lengthened out of angles and bulk. He had a lean, sinewy kind of strength, his tightly coiled muscles packed firm under his skin. No thick neck, bulging biceps, not like the other boys. People saw him as more fragile than his sister, with his delicate porcelain cheekbones and dewy blue eyes. Women on the street had called him *beautiful* instead of *handsome* since he was old enough to understand their cooing. Sylvy was stocky and strong. She looked better in trousers than Cecil did. She looked more of a man than he did. According to their father, Sylvy *was* more of a man than him.

To make matters worse, Cecil also looked like a pale weed next to Vernon, Sylvy's now-conscripted boyfriend. Vernon's hard, wide chest could crack a hand. He had let Cecil punch him once before – *Go on, hit me in the chest. It won't hurt.* Cecil laughed as the muscle flinched under the shirt, but Vernon showed no sign of pain. The two boys used to have fun. Those were the days before Sylvy started to strut around like a peacock, up and down the streets arm-in-arm with him; before Cecil had asked to join the Coshers – because that was what all the other kids had done when they left school at fifteen – and Vernon patted his cheek lightly and *ah*'d, told him to ask again when the hollows in his cheeks had filled out.

A hand clamped onto Cecil's skinny shoulder, almost knocking him over. Al, a friend. He breathed relief, then scolded himself for needing to do so. A hand, is that all it takes to scare him?

'What's *she* doing here?' Al asked, his grotty yellow teeth in Cecil's face. He still found himself unable to tell Al that no one liked it when he spoke so close to their faces, despite being friends since childhood and neighbours since birth.

'She's always hanging about here now. With her... whatever.'

'Her gang, you mean?'

'Don't call them that.'

'A little birdie told me...' Al continued, not listening '...that she's picked a fight with those girls across the Bridge. The Kings.' His breath smelled, but Cecil couldn't tell him that either.

'That's a load of rubbish... but I'm tickled now. I want to hear this,' Cecil mumbled as he shook off Al and moved closer to the girls, but not so close that Sylvy would see him. Call it morbid curiosity, he reasoned. If she was set on being an idiot, then he should at least know the extent of her idiocy and whether it was likely to be reflected back on him. It was a brotherly kindness to make sure she had not *fully* lost the plot. Sylvy made an embarrassment of them both. He felt for her; that she thought she was someone.

Char lifted herself up onto the glass lid of a pinball machine, and Sylvy followed suit, their mouths chattering. He could just about hear their conversation through the arcade din.

'…about Harry, she might look like nothing much, but she's got a whole load of nippers following her around like she's God,' Char said. 'Besides, if it comes to a fight, then who knows whether the Hackers will join them, along with any of the others.' She paused. 'Harry wants war now that you pulled your blade out on her, and after you lied about handing over the turf, she's mad—'

'We should *want* to fight them,' Sylvy interrupted. 'This turf's ours, isn't it? We took it, we own it. It belongs to the Seven Sisters, not that lot.' *It belongs to Vernon*, Cecil thought.

'We shouldn't poke the bear,' Char cut in. She crossed her arms, locking off her chest. 'We have the turf, let's keep it, and let Harry cool off.'

'She won't cool off. She's like Edie.'

The others grumbled around her; Char sighed.

'She was a right nasty piece of work.'

'Alright to look at, though,' one of the guys near them chipped in. 'A big dozy blonde,' another added, welcomed by laughs. Sisters interjected too, but Cecil heard only a mush of voices. Behind, his co-workers from the garage had grouped around another attraction involving a peep-hole. They called out to him and he shrank from their view, hiding behind a betting game. When he turned back to Sylvy, her voice had become more impassioned. He must have missed something.

'They want to come for all of our turf, we should come for all of theirs.'

'Not a chance.' Char shook her head before Sylvy had even finished speaking. She shunted herself off the pinball machine.

'We should do it, for the boys.' Sylvy paused, then jumped in as Char was about to speak. 'There's always Ouisa.'

'Absolutely bloody not!' Char shook her head. 'We can't.'

'We *can*. Louisa Gray is our ticket to the coppers. Her dad works on the council. It's like how the Hackers have friends on the inside. The Coshers never could but *we* could talk to Ouisa, remind her how she's *one of the girls* and all that, see if she can put in a good word with—'

'What do you not understand about *no*? Let's not forget who's in charge here.' Char's hard stare silenced Sylvy. 'We can't go to Ouisa in the middle of a war, it will look like a last-ditch. She's a ticket we can only use once.'

'That's what I'm saying. We use it *now*.'

'Shut up, Sylvy,' Sal snapped. 'You don't know what you're talking about. I went to The Kings Head, and I delivered that message—'

'What message?' Char nudged in. Her head flitted between Sylvy and Sal.

'It's nothing.'

'What message, Sylvy?'

'I wanted to let Harry know we mean business.'

'You're a right idiot, you know that?' Char began, about to chastise. Cecil smiled.

'If Harry wasn't completely mad before, then she is now,' Sal went on talking. 'I walked around the streets for hours trying to walk off the nerves. I couldn't. My skin was… *buzzing*. And did you hear what happened last night? At Roddy's Rink?'

'What?' Char asked.

'Bert got her foot broken.'

'How?'

'Not a clue, but the Kings did it to her. I know it. And if Harry smashed the foot off one of her own, then what's she going to do to *us*?'

'Classic Sal,' Sylvy smirked. 'A shadow would scare you.' Sal clenched her fist. Sylvy saw, smiling a little. The fist loosened.

'Sal's right. Harry's more dangerous than you think. We should be careful, or we'll get caught out,' Morgan added. Cecil knew Morgan from the garage, where she worked as one of the secretaries. Hot to burn, quick to flash.

'We can see them coming from a mile away,' Sylvy continued. 'There's no way that they'll touch the dance halls or the cinemas, those are ours. Tomorrow night, we make them ours.'

Cecil wondered whether she ever tired of the sound of her own voice. An itchy hatred rose up in him, flooding to the backs of his eyeballs. He was afraid of what would happen if all that hatred sloshed out. What would he do with it? Where would he put it?

'A vote, then,' Char proposed. She leaned against the wall. Cecil had been working up the courage to interrupt them, rehearsing phrases in his head that would scatter them. Each time the opportunity came for him to butt in, he backed down. Sidney eyed him from inside the glass box: *go on*. Before he knew it, he had tripped on his moment to intervene and the vote had begun.

Sylvy would learn to grow up eventually, Cecil's father had reassured him. She would realize the borders of her world, eventually. *Eventually* was starting to seem too distant.

He turned to Al.

'Let's get out of here, I'm bored.' If this was his afternoon, then he wanted himself in it.

'I was just about to look at this stunner one more time!' Al whined, as he slipped his penny into the feeder of the Grip-Teze. Cecil grabbed his collar and pulled him, still complaining, through thickets of people towards the glass door. He shouldered it open and burst out onto the busy street.

Women, hordes of them, walked towards him, with their breasts pointing forwards out of shirts and jumpers and coats – all aimed at him. *For* him. Whenever he was around Sylvy these days, and all her talk of territory, he felt that itch at the base of his skull, and there was only one way to scratch it.

'Cor, look at those,' Al grinned. He nudged Cecil and nodded his head towards a woman crossing the road. The wind tore at her skirt. He licked his lips to wet them and whistled. She jumped at the noise, then sped up and onwards around the corner, swivelling her neck to scowl at him as she tottered off. He knew she would be smiling the second she was out of view. Al laughed next to him.

Whatever Cecil had felt in the arcade – eavesdropping on his sister, creeped out by the lurid smile of Sidney, uncertain at the hand of the Grip-Teze while the others egged him on and laughed at him for pausing too long – it all slipped away. And he didn't even have to pay a penny for this. It was free.

The two of them prowled the street, women parting

around them. Al muttered comments about the girls as they passed, telling Cecil to lunge on one, to make his move. But Cecil was biding his time for the kill.

Through the heads and prams and canes and rubbish bins, a bleached-blonde halo popped up stark against the grey drizzle. She was walking past the Astoria cinema, which loomed on the corner, its garish pin-lights glittering. There was another head beside it, a bustle of brown curls. The girls were dressed like Sylvy – adorning their insecurity with baubles. Easy prey. Cecil drew closer, Al trailing behind.

He shoved his hands into his pockets and fell into a swagger, slouching backwards and loosening his joints, trying to look as if he didn't care whether his bones were attached to each other, like Vernon walked. He had watched Vernon perform this routine a hundred times.

Cecil knocked into the brunette, and his hand emerged from his pocket at the right time to steady himself against her breast.

'Oh, I'm terribly sorry, love.' He covered his mouth in mock shock, with the hand that had touched her. 'You should watch where you're going.'

The girl with the bleached hair sighed, rolled her eyes and snapped on her chewing gum.

'Harry, c'mon…' She started to walk off, but Al stood himself in front of her, wide-lipped and grinning.

'Did you get a good grab?' Harry asked, irritated, looking down at her chest. Not much there to grab.

'Hey, what's that supposed to mean?' Cecil looked at Al like she was crazy. Al had rehearsed the stunt with Cecil before. It worked every time, no matter how long it took.

'It means you did it to touch me up, didn't you?' Spikier, perhaps, than Cecil was accustomed to.

'Well, who wouldn't want to?'

'I bet you think you're really funny.' Harry shook her head, crossed her arms.

'I don't know about that. All I know is that you and your friend are beautiful and I think we should see each other again some time. Isn't she beautiful?' He turned to Al, who nodded.

'She's very beautiful, Cecil.'

'We don't have time for this,' Harry replied. 'Get out of the way, you're blocking the pavement.'

'What's that, baby?' He tried to bring himself back into focus. He was in control. He had to be. A laugh burst out of the other girl's mouth. Cecil flinched.

'There they are.' Harry pointed across the road, nudging her friend. A stunned Cecil followed her finger. It landed on Sylvy, chatting behind the glass wall of the arcade.

Cecil felt suddenly small, smaller than he had ever felt. Before he could edge out a word, the door of the penny arcade slammed open and Sylvy and her gang were spilling out, their eyes falling on the girls next to him. Pedestrians grumbled as the gang belted out the arcade and across the road, an orchestra of shoes – steel-toed pumps and loafers – charging towards him, or *past* him, he soon realized. Their prey had already run in the other direction, leaving Cecil and Al like loose string-ends on the pavement. When Sylvy rushed past, she shoved Cecil with her shoulder, knocking him against the wall.

'Sorry, didn't see you there.' She winked, heckling him as she walked backwards. 'Go on, go play your little game.'

Cecil stood there in silence, his hands limp at his sides. He let the Sisters run around him and chase the girls out of his sight.

Tony, 2017

Jeers ring out from a table of four men on the other side of the pub. Their target is a woman with a glass of water on the table in front of her. She's all slicked down, gelled hair, turtleneck, her phone resting on the table beside her. Only a ghost would come here to drink water, and for a moment I'm sure that's what she is – her skin so thin and translucent that I can see a blue bloodless vein crawling up the right side of her forehead; beady eyes scanning the room for other signs of un-life; itching the glass she's gripping loosely with her skinny-wristed hands. Her ghostliness wouldn't surprise me; things from the past lumped onto the table and into fellow seats are the order of the day. It's what I've come here for. The men continue joshing with her, and about the water, no less. She's visible, then.

She pulls the corners of her lips into her cheeks, giving the table of hecklers a tight half-smile, trying to act like she's in on the joke. But their persistence is impressive.

'A cheap date if that's all she drinks, lads,' the one facing me remarks. He follows it up with an absolute corker of a cough that makes everyone in the pub grimace.

She starts to gather up her things and readies them in her lap, preparing to dart off. Embarrassment blasts over her face. The hecklers start to tell her she doesn't have to leave, *love*.

It's stupid of me to intervene, but an old instinct surges up.

'Fancy some company, lovely?' I call out across the tables, half-standing. I thought my voice would be louder.

The men swivel in their seats. The woman looks up, scowling – at me.

'Oh, look, Mum's got involved now,' one of them laughs. Another hawking cough. I am old enough to be her mother – or grandmother.

'She's got a right to be left alone,' I nod. Harry would have hit them with a bin lid, a spare bit of fence, a small slice of war lying around.

'I'm fine,' the woman shakes her head, and directs a *can you believe this old bag?* look at the table of men. Her embarrassment directed towards me. I've made it worse for her, it's clear. Every man, and woman, for herself these days.

The red-faced, coughing one stands. He's clenching and unclenching his fist. He walks towards me; I freeze.

Stay put. At the last minute, he swerves around me, fist swinging past my ear, and heads to the bar. Some laughs burp out from the table, the woman included. Why would he waste a hit on me? I wonder whether to leave. It's still not too late, no one else is here. It would be like I had never arrived. No time wasted.

I took the underground to avoid the streets, but the nasty shock of surfacing was worse. That's not even to mention that old bones don't agree with the screeching and grinding on the rails, old ears don't agree with that voice dinging *This is Highbury and Islington.* More like *this is highly unbearable.* At least the passengers let up the priority seat now, even though the assurances keep coming that *you don't look a day over sixty, darling* when it's clear I look all eighty-one of my years. This is preferable, I suppose, to listening to the tinny heel-clicks walk themselves up the white-cream walls of an empty flat in Chelsea with its views and its marble and its pictures of myself on magazine covers. Every corridor in the flat is a hall of fame: *Life, Vogue, Hello, Fashion Weekly, Variety,* the Gucci campaign from the seventies, all versions of myself like reflections in funhouse mirrors I barely recognize.

This is Finsbury Park, and this helps me escape those halls of fame with my cover-selves covering themselves immodestly, staring at the little viney scar enlarged on my left cheek down to the jawline, the slash always spoiling the shoots, someone calling *cut* as they repositioned me to get another profile. The stories I've made up about that, as they made me up in the make-up chair and asked *where did you get that?* and I'd mumble about tripping over the ruins when I was a kid, change the subject, and start reciting the biography of the poor girl left behind in the Blitz while her friends went off on trains to the woodlands and greenlands. *Shitlands*, Harry had called them, to make me feel better about missing out on the distance that none of them ever appreciated enough.

I went through the routine a hundred times, because of the picture that became hot property among the press, because of what happened after it was taken. I was never afraid that fingers would come pointing at us, criminal proceedings, none of that. But they wanted to know what they wanted to know about us, and I delivered. A soundbite they could munch on with their tea. *There was very little hope living around there. It made us desperate really. We thought, well, we've got nothing to lose, there's no future for us.* They turned over bits of information like magpies, their eyes lit up when they heard that I occupied two rooms for which I could never make the rent, or that my neighbour's father died when she was eleven-or-so from a disease that most definitely could be cured today. *The things that went on in those rooms were tragic and sad, so we did our best to stay out of them.* The Cockney kid with lashes for days, that's all they needed.

It's your choice, the woman from the model agency told me on the phone in that first call. But what choice did I have, really: there were no decent jobs in Islington for girls like us. I ran from the memories and into the spiky elbows of other girls who weren't allowed to eat, taking notes on how to sit, how to get out of a car with my knees pressed firmly together, the correct way to walk with stomach in and pelvis forwards, learning, learning, learning.

Learning the hard way, I suppose, after a discreet sacking – *dismissal*, they called it – when I smacked a designer with wandering hands and deliberately tore up the skirt I should have been honoured to wear for him. *I don't care if it's what you learned on the streets or not, it won't get you to Paris*, the other models told me. As his hand touched the smooth skin of my shin and started to work its way upwards, and he was telling me how he hated it when European women refused to shave their legs, I turned to see if anyone was there for back-up – just seven other models glad that his hands were not on their legs, none willing to intervene to take his hands off mine. Silent sisters, tottering on the spot in their heels. The only friendship I knew was between my tonsils and my two pokey fingers; the taste of my fingerprints all the way at the back of my throat.

The designers and scouts pitted us against each other like chickens in a cockfight; we were too busy fighting each other to fight the men who were placing bets on us at the fashion shows. Which one would fall first. Which one would fall into their beds first. Which ration-skinny kid could they get into their echoey penthouse with its powders and needles. I started to wonder how I would survive as a solo army, once they started snapping me into billboards that lined streets I'd never seen and called me Toni Adams and called me *The Face of '61* in magazines my family never read. When I let the designers touch all parts of me, I remembered Harry's touch on my shoulder, the urgency in her eyes. The feeling of dying for each other, as I realized that I would die for none of these plastic girls. The bloodied teeth of the girl I dragged down the stairs for her Prada heels and her spot on the catwalk. I had been spoiled with Harry; it spoiled everything that came after. I acted like I had nothing to lose – I had already lost it.

Chasing the tail of Harry, I wound through acres of new tunnel to emerge from the underground station – only to be greeted by shiny glass office buildings, an expensive cinema, two Starbucks. Steps from the station, pasty lads in a pub garden were singing *oh, Jeremy Corbyn* to 'Seven Nation Army'. Further down Blackstock, a Jewish bakery, a Turkish kebab shop, a Romanian supermarket, a Uyghur deli, a Polish butcher, a mishmash and mania of ish. On the slat of pavement where there was now a Lidl, Harry had sworn that she'd defend her English soil from the Germans, whatever it took, if that meant her life. *The Jerries are gone for now, but it's only a matter of time*, she fumed, terrifying and exciting us at once. She could swear for England, we said.

On the next corner, I flinched at the boy in blue – although they're not all boys and they're not in blue anymore, but in black, with black-and-white chequered chessboard stripes, with no chess pieces, Kevlar-heavy, armed to the teeth on their patrol near the station, no longer local bobbies.

We thought the streets would never change. But look at that, they did, changed and called us collateral. All that energy we tipped here, where did it go? Slipped into the cracks between the delicatessens and the DIY shops, pavement cracks ripped up and re-pasted a hundred times over since our steel-toed shoes coloured them ours. Blue plaques dot the brick-fronts with names and dates of birth, but none of them are ours. It took everything I had not to get back on the train and head south.

The school and its green gates, still there, should have a blue plaque commemorating the day that Harry took a cricket bat to the face, the day that we met. Harry, my darling, sweet Harry, awful Harry, Harriet to her mother, swaggered towards me at lunch, took my marbles and called me Curly Crisp. I couldn't dye my hair properly then, the Marilyn Monroe shade came out piss-yellow, and after a home perm it would frizz and wire itself into ugly springs hugging my scalp, making me look like a cheap dolly. I asked for the marbles back. Resounding *No. Unbloodybelieveable*, I thought. *Why don't you take them back*, Harry's eyes challenged. I wasn't going to take that. I went home with new resolve: I wasn't going to let a kid like that make a fool of me. No, I had to build myself another limb – my brother's bat. It would do more good than a mouth, more good than talk. A good cosh, that'd do it. I'd have a nice conversation with Harry that lasted for two cricket-bat thwacks.

I shoved the bat in my jacket and walked to school like it was a part of me, a thick rib grown outside the skin. Then at lunchtime, right there near the gates, I thwacked Harry on the shins. She went straight down. I asked for an apology. Nothing. Another thwack to the face. Harry smiled and the blood dyed those teeth scarlet. *Don't come near me again*, I said, as threateningly as I could. Harry could have screamed bloody murder, but when someone asked who the attacker was, she smiled and showed her rusty red teeth and shot off a lie about Marcus, the boy with the big coat. *Why did you lie?* I asked her after school, when she was kicking rubble outside the gates. She didn't answer my questions, then or ever, and launched into explanations of some *agreement* she had. *If one of us is in trouble, she whistles for a King. And if a King isn't there, then she will be soon. It's your choice. You're in, Tony.* I tried to tell her it was Antonia but she told me it was *just Tony from now on* and it was from then on. That was Harry; her way went. I was in.

All of N4 was heavy with deadweight memory as I tracked the route to the pub. Who would suppose that these hipster-stained streets set the scene for one of the dirtiest gang rivalries in the fifties, no one but me is asking. The streets have had a hip replacement – at least this far from the station. This end of Blackstock forgot to talk to the end with Jewish bakeries and Polish butchers. Mr Shiney's, our favourite spot to shoplift cigarettes, has become a pottery painting bar, charging seventeen quid for a plain bowl they then make you paint. A bookshop sells coffee and wine and croissants. There used to be a gap where the Green-Fusion restaurant sits; some idiot had burned down a laundrette on Guy Fawkes Night, a firework working itself down the streets, screaming at head height to plant itself in the first-floor bedroom.

The pavements now full of little girls with wet, newly washed hair who walk beside their mothers, clasping ready hands. A white-shirted and blue-jeaned father perched on a dinky pastel chair at an outdoor table, flanked by his two children – *is that smoothie nice, Vivi?* he asked, and she smiled in answer. He started to direct them, waving them cheek to cheek with his hand, *come on, let's take a photo for Mummy*, and his daughter's arm toppled the gunky purple drink, thick with seeds. A surprising irritation came over him as he snatched napkins and scraped the puddle onto the floor; smushed at the liquid clotting her dress. *That was silly wasn't it, Vivi?* These are the sorts of things that ruin days here now.

At another kerbside table, a baby screamed beside her mama from white terraced house *number three* in white sipping her flat white – and straight away it was nineteen-fifty-something again and the plot's all ruined rafters and black charcoal. Harry had screamed to *Get the cam'ra!* Someone replied, *What you want that for?* Then my voice, laughing, *Just git it!* But, *I said what for!* The reply: *To snap this!* The snap that broke me into a career, after someone saw me dressed in snappy suit, neckscarf and net hat, traced me and called me, and asked me if I wanted to *make it to Paris.*

A lighter snapping on the corner of Blackstock, near the pub. Three kids – one older, proudly bearing his pencil-line moustache and a rolled joint hanging from his mouth, and two younger ones sucking on vapes between unsure glances at each other. They bumped fists, and small plastic bags exchanged hands and were folded into pockets. The younger kids' eyes followed the older one's every movement; they copied the way he stood, the cigarette puff, the way he rolled the money into a tight cylinder and slid it down his sleeve, those little understudies preparing for their roles in the paper, studying under the grand masters without a care for their mothers, mothers weeping, understudies all the way to the grave. What was the boy from last week called? Police tape still flutters near the mosque.

Last night, I dreamt I went to The Kings Head again; again, the owner stood behind the bar, polishing pint glasses with her wrist bending in that unholy angle; again, Saint's wrist skittered along a piece of paper, drawing up schemes; again, the twins planned how to get that boy with the greasy hair into the bathroom without his girlfriend noticing; again, I noticed Harry's every edge, the nub of a cigarette turning her lips to slivers of ash, her hair stiff with pins, eyes black as a cat's and charming, and the edge was hers, the room was hers, Harry, who stood at the bar, Saint polishing her glasses in the mirror, smiling at the owner, smiling at me, smiling at the room.

In the dream, the white paint peeled in ribbons, the red awning flaked to the ground, the outdoor tables in the beer garden buckled and bulged like belts on Sunday, rained out, reined in, bursting their seams, panels out of shape and wobbly. It was nothing without us. Nothing but a wreck, our wreck, our lovely living wreck. Nothing like this – newly painted and unfamiliar, not as we left it. The coolness of pool balls replaced by the stench of paint and stale piss; our newspaper cuttings tossed for television screens with football matches. Leeds vs Man United.

I trace beads of condensation slipping down the sides of the glass and disappearing into the wood, a smugness rising: the pub won't be theirs for much longer either. We convinced ourselves it was ours, but the old woman who ran the place never put up that apostrophe after the s – *because it's ours, our Head* – not for a lack of begging. Probably took it to the grave, knowing her. I always thought it looked like the beginning of a sentence: The Kings head into battle, The Kings head towards you, The Kings head to the doorstep of prosperity. We never ran the place on paper, but we had reigned here as Kings, reigned over the world we created for ourselves.

I guess it doesn't matter if people remember me as *The Face of '61* if no one remembers that I used to nick from the backs of lorries beside Harry or that I cut my arms on rhinestones from stolen dresses or that she lit my cigarettes for me when I couldn't afford matches or that she swiped my hip flask sometimes to keep me sober and

I pretended I didn't notice. This pub is the last chess piece between us and checkmate – complete oblivion. That whole world of ours sliding off the shelf, and no one will even notice when it's gone.

Following my attempted intervention, I become the elephant in the room as the men continue to drink and comment on the younger woman and the football interchangeably.

The door opens, and someone budges in, rushing. There's no need to turn and look.

'Sorry I'm late. These guys bothering you?'

Saint puts her coat on the back of the chair and sits down, the warmth on her face almost enough to make me cry.

SEVEN

The Kings, crowded around a door propped open with a concrete block, were trying to get into Harfleur Hall. The problem was their clothes. A crude sign stuck to the front entrance read YOUTHS WEARING EDWARDIAN DRESS WILL NOT BE ADMITTED. All the dance halls and hotels – and most cinemas, too – had started to put these up; backhands in the blocky font of newspapers, etched with the fear that the kids in coloured velvet collars and cuffs, trousers so tight they couldn't sit and long narrow ties like bootlaces, would intrude on their peaceful passing of time. Everything was on course, finally, after the war and the last thing they needed was another bomb to counterblast their evenings. Tony, with a net hat perched on top of her tightly wound arrangement of platinum blonde hair, had taunted the doormen, saying she could take off her shirt if that was what it took. Leslie even got so far as to strip her blazer and wave it around her head, attracting the attention of some bystanders. After some talk, Saint convinced her to put it back on and the Kings headed to the dead-ended alley behind, with its bins and tins and old signs, where a siege was now occurring at the stage door.

The dance hall, in disputed territory, stood on a worn cusp of street. Central to Islington, invisible when the sun shone, it boomed at night. The stone palace bundled up under-thirties in sweaty, over-thirty-degree air, which spilled out and collided with the cold clamp of the street. Jazz and rock 'n' roll swelled over the terraced houses nearby.

Saint turned from the doorway and swatted Tony's arm, hissing:

'Where's Harry? It's gone nine, she should be here by now.'

Tony shrugged – and Saint turned back to the half-open door, arguing with whomever was on the other side of it. Rain tipped on them, and puddles in the alley quivered with the energy of rustling feet as the crowd milled about itself, little ants crawling along plates. They needed Harry, to realign and pull them out of scatter.

Harry – Tony knew – was off doing something that almost certainly wouldn't work. She was rock-n-rolling with an old lover in his bed, trying to fill herself up with him. A transaction that never quite paid off. She knew far too much about Harry's sex life, Tony thought, shaking her head; she had started to keep the secrets even Harry kept from herself. But she had agreed to her simple *you know why I'll be late.* Just as she had agreed to join her behind the cricket shed years ago and agreed to venture with her to the other side of the Bridge the day before to scout out Harfleur Hall, despite the drizzle most certainly turning her hair to frizz.

While Saint pleaded with the man at the back door, Tony polished her face in the dirty window. It was as symmetrical as two sides of a knife, a perfect, pale oval. Prodding her skin, she evened out the powdered drabs like finger-painting a blank canvas, trying to keep her hands busy. She grimaced at the grey shawls under her eyes, from where she had spent the previous night drumming her fingertips on the windowsill and watching the sunrise hint itself into being. After their chase on the Sisters' turf, her heartbeats still raced each other, pumping taut, baby-fresh blood into her ears in slick and silent beats. The thrill of it shot her onto a high and charged her hands; she forgot about the nerves. Her feet had slapped Seven Sisters Road, sending judders to the base of her skull, and the hip flask had remained in her pocket.

Tony would forever be grateful to Harry for that quickening sensation; she would forever love her for the hours she'd kept Tony from her empty rooms and their potential for boredom – but those hours had added and added into years, and the high was turning stale. Their quips and sayings were sagging and starting to stare back at Tony. *There are no decent jobs for girls our age here*, their mantra, was now beginning to beg the question in her brain, *why don't you go somewhere else, then?* In Harry's two-month absence, she had started to realize that she was solely Harry's Tony, no one in her own right. A witness that couldn't change her story, or else. When Harry had informed her that she was no longer called Antonia on these streets, *just Tony*, then she ditched her name and corrected anyone who told her different – including the teacher who had stopped her last week as she left the darkness of the Astoria. *Antonia!*

She found herself, there between the kerb and the yellow line. The teacher asked whether she was on her way to Paris yet. Tony assumed it was some kind of mix-up before she remembered that she had fantasized over Paris with Mrs Patrick at the back of the textiles classroom. A book on fashion still lingered somewhere at the back of her bedroom, an outstanding loan that she had never returned. Stuck short of a reply, she had made excuses and skittered off in the other direction from Mrs Patrick, terror crowding her chest. The last thing she needed was to remember the past and its potentials. Harry was the strongest alcohol Tony had ever tried. The best at making her forget. She could never swear off drink; she could never swear off Harry.

'What if Harry doesn't show?' Saint murmured at her. 'Shall we call it a night? Come back next week?'

'Saint, trust me, she's on her way,' Tony said. 'Stop wittering on.'

'Look, we've got to do this tonight. Even if we have to storm the place,' Jackie offered.

'*Storm*?' Saint's eyes widened at Jackie's suggestion – namely, at the fact that she had started to make them. Since Bert had been cut, there was a vacuum that needed filling. The twins had muscled in. 'There's one thing for certain and it's that Harry's going to have to pull a miracle out of her pocket to convince them to let us in.' Saint set her mouth and plucked a cigarette from behind her left ear, thinking it a pencil, and bit down hard. With a *phew phew*, she spat the tobacco off her tongue and brushed it frantically off her clothes.

For tonight, she wore a carefully casual lint-rolled suit, with her pinned hair expertly manipulated into tough beauty. The Kings had dressed well, but with an inkling that all might not stay in place. They had fastened themselves for a night of movement, with little hairspray clouds on shoulders and shirts tucked in securely. The writings of nervous fingers and absent minds in stray hairs and jacket creases.

Jackie gestured her head to one of the umbrellas in the makeshift courtyard, under which stood some younger girls.

'Are you worried about them?'

'What, about Harry? Well, I'm always worried about Harry.'

'No, about the kids. *Them.*'

'Kids,' Tony laughed. 'They're not much younger than you and Les.'

'You know what I mean.'

Saint shook her head.

'They'll be fine. They're just excited to be here. Remember when you first came to a dance hall, a proper dance hall?' Saint's eyes sparkled with the memory. 'I was late, and I've never forgotten it. I rushed over and wormed my way in and…' she breathed out. 'It was a hell of a lot of fun. Edie was there. Edie would never mix dancing with business. They were separate in Edie's book. And they're separate in mine. I don't like the idea of doing this on a Saturday night. We should have done it in the afternoon when it's quiet, somewhere we can control the stakes… The kids will follow our lead. Just like we did with Edie, remember?' Saint smiled at the thought. 'Look at them. Green as untrampled grass.'

'What's the wait all about?' Nell moaned, arms crossed and teeth chattering. Her foot tapped and splashed the ground in a jittery waiting dance. The three huddled under Petie's wide umbrella.

'Keep your wig on,' Petie offered as a reply. 'We're lucky just to be here.'

'Except we're not really *here*, are we? Nothing feels lucky about standing in the freezing rain.'

'You can't see the fun in anything, Nell. Bernie understands, don't you, Bernie?' Upon hearing her name, Bernadette nodded.

'And where's Harry?' Nell continued. She watched Saint and Tony glance around and keep their eyes on the street – everyone was on display tonight.

'The other Kings look worried.' Bernadette gritted her teeth. '*I'm* worried.'

'We *should* be worried. This isn't our spot… it's theirs.'

'Shut it, Nell. Lighten up. Let your hair down. Or I'll let it down for you.' Nell squinted at Petie's lips, examining whether the quirk was a threat. 'You're the one that wanted to be a King. You're the one that roped us into all this, and I've got to say… I'm starting to like it.' Petie hadn't quite been the same since the night on the doorstep; her tears had crystallized, hardened. After Harry made them Kings, she had started speaking in ultimatums too perfect to sound like real speech: *I'll be a King or I'll die.* Thinking of the Kings opened up sinkholes in her head.

'I just want to dance,' Bernadette said. She grabbed her skirts and gave them a *whish-wash* in the night, creating a little breeze under the umbrella. 'If there's dancing then all is right in the world… right?'

The rain started to fall harder. Nell grabbed her twig-arms and hugged tighter.

'They're only a bit older than us.' Petie looked to Saint and the twins on the other side of the alley. 'Just think, a couple years and we'll be where they are.'

'Sometimes I forget about getting older. It's nothing silly,' Bernadette replied to Petie's snigger. 'But when I get so wrapped up in the shop, in just day-to-day doing what's what, I forget that I'm getting older every second—'

'She's here,' Petie cut Bernadette's rambles short.

A black cut-out walked down the alley, lamplight shining the outline into view. Saint yelled something across the wet night. The figure stuck an arm up in greeting. Flashes of pearl and faux gold hit the wet brick walls as the Kings checked and re-checked their clutches for the lipsticks they already knew were there.

'If I'd known it would be so difficult to get in the door, I wouldn't have—' Saint began.

'Did you ask for the owner?' Harry interrupted as she arrived in the alley.

'What good would that do?' Saint hissed, carefully out of earshot of the kids. 'Look, he won't let us in. He doesn't want trouble. I tried to tell him that we wouldn't be trouble, but he won't—'

'Who says we have to be *let* in?'

'You're suggesting...' Saint trailed off.

'Don't get your posh knickers in a twist, Saint. We'll ask him, *much* nicer than we did before.' Harry let Saint catch up.

'We'll bribe him?'

Harry nodded, gesturing for her to fill in the rest of the plan. '...but the others won't know.' Saint leaned into the door once more and asked for the owner.

Tony inspected the awaiting Harry. She wore a full, cream-coloured skirt, coupled with a black polo neck and a string of fake pearls. Tony could see how chock-full her clutch was, bulging with spare lipstick, powder, combs, and a careful choice of weapons: blades stuck down linings, a knuckle clasp and, most crudely, a sock stuffed with coins. Harry would beat her opponent with the Queen's face if necessary.

'How was it?' Tony asked after a while, discreet. Harry sniffed the cold evening air.

'Disappointing.' She paused, inspecting Tony. 'You look tired.'

Tony went to reply, but the door swung open. A withered man stood inside, leaning against the wall: Gov. The inner corridor dwarfed his thin frame, all sinew and weathered twine twisted up into a near-bent stick of a man, his collarbones protruding through the back of his shirt like chicken wings. He drew fast drags on a cigarette, barely inhaling or exhaling any smoke. His arm continued pulling it to and from his lips, even when Harry stepped up to the doorway. The gentle scent of music wafted out the door.

In a gradual slowing of the cigarette-pulling, he squinted. Then he began the steady motion again: dragged, heaved, dragged, heaved.

'You're girls,' he observed between drags.

Harry looked herself up and down. 'I think so.'

Gov peeped out to inspect the twenty-or-so others in the alley. He scratched his head, and wound his neck back in.

'No, it's just… I'm a bit confused, that's all.' He paused, expecting her to validate his confusion. 'The hall manager said there was a load of Teds out the back trying to get in and that I was to go and talk some sense into them. I assumed he meant… *Teds*, you know.' She knew. 'You can't blame me.' He gestured to Harry and the others.

'No, you're right,' Harry responded. 'And looking like this, most people would think that we are Teds, so you can't blame your hall manager either.'

Gov nodded.

'Violence, all that, it's not a thing for girls.' He went on, scrunching his forehead into a wad of brown paper. 'You're not with those fellas I just threw out, are you?'

'Which fellas?'

'One of them collectives... hooligans. The ones the papers love.' He seemed primed to launch into a tirade on *the papers*. 'One lot of them took over a ballroom up in Bradford the other week. I read about it. From the photos, it looked like a fucking bomb had hit the place.' He covered his mouth. 'I shouldn't use that language in front of ladies, should I?'

Harry felt she was expected to answer.

'It's alright, Gov. We've heard a lot worse.'

'I expect you have... hanging around with lads like those. What do you want then? Are you looking to come in?' he asked, waving a hand behind him, towards the music. 'Because I can't have you coming in dressed like Teds, and any of those boys following you in here, destroying the place.'

Harry raised an eyebrow.

'How about...' Harry placed one foot forwards, onto the step. Gov stepped back, then steadied himself, a little surprise on his face. 'How about we come in, as we are, we dance and we have a good time.' It wasn't a question. Gov made no move. 'You're right. Violence, that sort of behaviour, it's not for girls. We're just looking to have a right laugh.'

'You *are* Teds, then.'

'Look, I get it,' Harry said, keeping back irritation in her voice. 'It's a real head scratcher. We're Teds, but we're not.' Some of the girls snorted laughs behind her. 'Let's agree to disagree, alright? Or we'll be going back and forth about it all night. I think we can move on to… other matters now.'

He took a long drag of his cigarette, considering.

'How much, Gov?'

'For what?'

'For the lot of us to come in this back door.'

Gov swallowed with a grim grin, his Adam's apple bobbing.

'Twelve.'

'Ten,' Harry whispered.

'Eleven.'

'*Ten.*'

'Fork it over, then.'

Harry dug in her clutch and handed over the paper and coins like they were nothing but scraps of cloth and old buttons. Gov fingered the money with tender care and clasped them tight. After a final drag, he put out his cigarette next to Harry's feet and disappeared into the belly of the hall, the door left open behind him.

*

Harry emerged from the doorway, smiling.

Her voice jumped up in volume as she announced to her crowd of Kings: 'What are you waiting for?'

Petie left the umbrella's petty shade, as if the canopy would somehow block Harry's rays of speech. Entranced, mumbling yeses, she stood in her rain-spattered future. Nell and Bernadette remained underneath.

'After tonight, this dance hall will be ours,' Harry declared. 'We're taking it, and there's nothing the Seven Sisters can do about it, eh?' Harry's voice clanged about the small courtyard. 'There are old faces here, and new faces... but they're Kings' faces. Go in there and show them what the Blackstock kids, the Terrace kids, can do. Teach them how to dance. Spirit and body. That's all it takes. A little spirit and a little body. Fan out. Follow your instincts. Play your games. Have your dances. But *no* fighting. I'll be dealing with the business end. And if I say scram, I mean it. For Finsbury Park, and...' Harry's voice dropped '...and Mr George.'

The group hooted against the night.

'I'd die for Harry,' Petie vowed. Nell and Bernadette passed each other sceptical looks.

The Kings began to move as one towards the door. Puddles splashed, umbrellas reeled in like fishing rods, and the door banged against the outside brick wall, struck into a match-flame of energy. Harry ushered through the current of grey-backed kids, teenagers, twenty-somethings. The door shook on its hinges.

Petie and Nell, closely followed by Bernadette, were the final few stragglers, trying to remain attached members. Harry playfully slapped them on the arms as they crowded in, looking for action. She lingered at the door, hanging her head in the night – far from the swelling music. Tony slackened in the corridor, turning to her leader as she had done time and time before:

'Are you coming, Harry?'

EIGHT

'Would you look at that!' The tunnel spat Petie into the centrifugal, twisting churn of the dance floor, where colours melted and boldened, hardened and melted, blood-red dresses dancing with slate-grey suits. Mint-green sleeves held pale-pink arms wrapped in tresses of fake pearl. With hot, high, bouncy air, the hall could have been thousands of feet above the earth, but for the hundreds of slams to the beat on the polished wooden floor, drumming the spot into the minds of those who tapped and creeped and swirled and swapped and tumbled and lifted. Mirrors lined the walls, duplicating the room's size and doubling the number of dancers; a multitude of selves abounded.

The music swung limberly one moment and teetered into rock-a-beatin'-boogie the next, with the bodies shifting and changing gears like cars careening around the streets in the dead of night. Yellows and ambers bathed the dancers in pure movement, the air radiating with stage light. There were no windows and no shadows. Limbs protruding, some of them bare and some covered, backsides, frontsides, all on show, because this was Saturday night. Virgins clutched their bags tight, giggling if someone said *hi*. Little groups crusted in corners around elbow-high tables, sipping on drinks, waiting to be picked up and jacked and taken out for a spin.

From their foot-high stage, the band controlled the room's temperature, a force of mercury with tired tongues and lips and fingers red with welts. Sweating with power, their rose-red faces hovered about the instruments like accessories, barely taking breaths as the room swept them up. They ruled the night – before their cased-up instruments had to lie tired in the corner of their bedsits.

Petie wanted to watch every dancer at the same time and absorb every sight at once, a child too impatient to chew on its food. She tried to digest the hall corner by corner instead, and the fizz of wonder seeped through her limbs – along with the evening's readiness for danger. Her eyes drifted to the exit, but who was she kidding? Petie knew she would see it through. She was a King now.

With Nell and Bernadette grumbling beside her, Petie panned across the room, sticking to the sides, slipping past backs. She watched hands curl under tabletops to grip fingers and stroke lazy palms and slide down thighs and under skirts and undo belt buckles to slip in a finger or two. Harry caught her eye in the mirror and swivelled to face the trio.

'You three,' she turned on them. 'Do me a favour.'

'Anything.' Petie drank in the leader's request.

'You're my eyes and ears.' Harry raised her voice over the music. 'I can trust you three, can't I? If you see the Sisters, if anyone gives you any funny business, come find me.' Harry patted Petie's forearm. The younger King went to open her mouth once more, but a cold blast of air flew into the hall from the front entrance and Seven – give or take – Sisters whirled in. The music stepped up a notch to fast beats and the hunky-dory voices sang louder; a blue guitar riff cooled the room.

'Speak of the devil,' Tony muttered nearby.

Sylvy was flushed with drink and the cold night, her hair awry from the wind. Her eyes scanned the room before landing on Harry. They narrowed in fury.

'She's on time.' Harry looked at her watch. 'What did I say? If Sylvy heard that we were here, and before her, then she'd show up, she'd cause a fuss. She'll do something stupid, and the hall will be ours. Bob's your uncle.'

The Sisters ploughed through the crowds of dancers towards Harry, who used the mirror-clad walls to look without looking. The suits clomped themselves around her bubble of Kings in an unwelcome welcome.

'What do you think you're doing here?' Char crossed her arms. Petie had to remind herself once more that she was the one who led the Seven Sisters and not Sylvy.

'We're here for a dance on our turf.' Harry turned into a smirk on legs.

'What makes you think you own this side of the Bridge?' Sylvy leaned in. 'That you can even show your face this side of the Bridge. This is *our* hall.'

'Sure.' Harry looked behind her and saw one of the doormen wave his hand at the air; he couldn't be bothered to chase girls.

'This is the best dance hall in town,' Tony chipped in.

'You've never felt the need to dance here before. Have they run out of music in whatever hall you usually go creeping around?'

'All the music in the world, all the music I want to hear, is under this roof.'

'You should leave.' Char's ears were red. 'There are too many people here, too many that aren't involved.' Her eyes flicked to Petie, who still hung onto the gathering.

A microphone twanged through the air; Harry stepped back a foot, while some reached for their ears. A sudden silence fell; the dancers' shoe squeaks on the polished parquet the only conversation.

'Allllright everybody!' The bandleader's thorny ram-shackle throat hawked into the microphone. He oozed showmanship. 'We're going to be trying something different, something all the kids are doing across the pond in the U S of A.'

The hall came to a momentary stop, like a broken carousel. Dancers let out some half-trusting whoops and cheers. Petie kept her eyes fixed on the Sisters.

'It's called a ladies' excuse-me dance.' The room fizzed with excitement. 'The rules are simple. Ladies, you begin the dance with a partner, and the second another girl comes up to you, taps your shoulder, and says *excuse me*, then you've got to dance with their handsome partner, while your partner dances with them. No ifs, no buts, no coconuts.'

The saxophone screeched into life. Couples sprang up from the polished wood and began one-stepping, two-stepping, tap-stepping and hop-skipping to a tune so fast that it struggled to keep up with itself.

'One dance, Sylvy. One dance, and then we can figure out who owns this joint.'

'One dance and then you *leave*.' Their voices scuffled to get above the band's clashing rip-roar and the bodies of those already engaged and excuse-me-ing were bumping into them at odd intervals. Harry's eyes had begun scanning the crowd for a potential partner as she spoke. Sisters and Kings began coring off, mulching into the general mass, which throbbed in time to the saxophone frills. Petie, too, subsumed herself in the dancing mob.

'There's too many of them.' Char nodded to Sylvy as she picked a partner.

'They're everywhere, fiddly little pricks... bar, cloak-room, floor.' Sylvy gritted her teeth, and tapped on the shoulder of the closest man. 'She's even got kids involved. Look at the bar, I recognize that lot from the Terrace.'

Sylvy kept watch on Harry and her lengthening trail of discarded partners; every few moments, she tapped someone's shoulder and swooped in to break up another couple. Jiving legs and loose arms stuck out through the melee. She swapped and excuse-me'd her way around the entire dance hall. Half-awed, half-disgusted, Sylvy wondered why Harry had to have absolutely everything. Why the hall; why the Sisters' territory?

The Coshers' territory, she corrected herself. Too often now, Sylvy was forgetting that she was merely house-keeper of the turf while Vernon and the other boys were away. It would be hard to grow out the habit of acting like she owned it. The excitement and ambition in taking on the Kings – taking their streets – had ambushed her. All of a sudden, when she kicked a King into the gutter and stole from their shop, she felt good. And when she took one street, she wanted to take two more. When she took those two, she wanted four. After she had four, she wanted eight. The exponential fever overtook her like jam over bread. The more Char discouraged her, warning her about the Coshers and what Vernon would think, the more she was encouraged. It was all for him, of course, she told Char and she told herself, but believing that was becoming harder.

Harry searched the dance floor for Sylvy, hoping that she was watching on. If she was a flame, then Harry intended to stoke her.

Someone was heckling Harry to the left: Tony. She had tapped the shoulder of a pimply kid nearby who seemed unimpressed that he was the vehicle for her to get close enough to Harry for a conversation. Jackie, meanwhile, brushed their backs, trying – failing – to catch Harry's eye.

'Sylvy's breathing fire,' Tony shouted over the music, and over her partner's shoulder.

'That's because we're winning.'

'Don't get cocky, we've just had a little invasion, that's all.'

'Then let's make the most of it. If this was ours, Tony... then there's free rein.' Harry grinned. 'Think how much fun we could have here, riling up Gov, the back rooms, the balcony. You thinking of it?' Tony nodded. 'I can feel it already.'

A strong current of dancers pushed them apart, and Harry soon unclasped her current man and fell into another. Her feet ground the floor into mincemeat. A salty tang of sweat from a hundred necks and flailing forearms blended in the air, sweetened with hair wax. Hairspray glided into the dance hall on tracks of altitude from the powder room. Senses broke down into beats and *one-two-three-four*, *a-one-two-three-four*, and harmonies rose and fell like a wagging tongue. Clammed hands caught starched shirts, waists were gripped and moved, and hips were hand-holds used to swing harder, propel harder, groove west, or creep north. Harry closed her eyes and danced hard enough to pop eyeballs out the back of her skull, quick jives and jabs – hard enough to jolt out of her skin, become mere form bustling.

A high-pitched laugh trailed through the music and she flicked open her eyes. Where did she know that laugh from? If it was this side of the Bridge, then it was unlikely to be friendly.

Sylvy's brother – Harry couldn't remember his name – was encrusted with two others at the corner of the dance floor, half-turned away from her. There was one more chorus of the song, enough for a dance. Quickly, before

Tony could stop her, Harry ditched her current partner and strode towards him, breaking all the bandleader's rules by choosing someone not already on the dance floor. She patted him on his shoulder, demure, polite. He started to open his mouth, but she shunted – only half-playfully – at his chin, to shut it like a puppet's.

'Shh.' She lugged him by the hand onto the dance floor, the adrenaline washing away with the safety of all these other bodies.

'You know that my sister calls this *her* territory? Not that that means anything, of course,' Cecil blurted. 'It's all just make-believe.' Cecil narrowed his eyes; Harry rolled hers in return and led the dance. He continued trying to talk at her as she twirled and wound herself around him.

'We'll be calling this our territory soon enough,' she whispered near his ear, as the final chorus raged.

'You know, you should be more careful, Harriet, or something might happen.'

'You're the one that should be *careful*. Have you looked around lately? There are Kings in every corner of this place, and we're taking it tonight, whether your sister likes it or not.'

'Not this again,' Cecil huffed in disbelief. 'Sylvy's far enough gone, she doesn't need pushing over the edge with all this nonsense about wars and—'

'Now you're not just calling it nonsense because you don't have any gang of your own, are you? That would be a bit embarrassing, wouldn't it?'

'Oh, you arrogant… you shouldn't talk to me like that.'

'Why not, it's fun, to see your cheeks go all red. To know it's that easy.'

'You're a right nasty piece of work, you know that?'

'That's the best kind to be.' Harry grinned. The song was nearly over, and she backed up from him, searching for Sylvy's black hair. Where was an enemy when you needed her? 'You think I really wanted to dance with a miserable sap like you? Hanging around at the edges, a little *creep*, with nothing better to do than pretend to bump into girls. I can bump into people too.'

Cecil looked around him for an ally, for one of his friends, a Cosher, but there was no one. There were only Kings. Harry shoved her shoulder against him and he stumbled backwards into Tony, who pushed him back towards Harry with an *oi, watch it!*

On cue, Sylvy rushed in, grappling her brother like a loose buckle.

'Don't mess around with him,' she fumed.

'Why not, Sylvy?' Harry asked. Enraged, Sylvy pushed off her brother, hissing *get out of here*, and turned to Harry. She shoved her with both palms and the King lost her footing. Tony rushed in; Char pushed her back.

'If you knew what was good for you, you'd get out of here too.'

A microphone twang chewed down the end of the song, and the bandleader thanked everyone for their cooperation.

'I think it's time for you to leave,' Harry announced. Sylvy grabbed her shirt, walking her towards the wall. Kings drew to them. Sisters rushed over. The epicentre of Harfleur Hall changed from the dance floor to its sidelines. Harry tried to throw off Sylvy's hand, and both fumbled near the breast, breathless.

'Stop it,' a reedy voice cut through their squabble. Heaves and huffs came before their bodies, and Gov broke them up. 'You said there wouldn't be trouble,' he directed to Harry.

'She's the one causing it.'

'Liar,' Sylvy spat.

'Come with me, both of you.'

Sylvy let go of Harry and held her hands out in mock surrender. The Kings and the Sisters melted back into the corridors.

Gov rested his head in his hands.

'I don't understand why you kids can't leave it *be*. There's no *deal* on the table here. I just know that I can't have both of you... *collectives* in here at the same time. What does it matter who thinks they own the hall? I'm the landlord here. I own it.' He jammed his thumb into his sternum over and over. 'Why am I even having this conversation?'

'Because...' Harry jumped in, 'Because if you *don't* then—'

'Are you about to threaten me?'

'I wouldn't dream of it, Gov. I want to compliment your dance hall. It's the best.'

He nodded in approval. The room was crammed: six Kings offset seven Sisters. Dark-wood panelling fenced them in. Gov sat upright in his chair, sandwiched in a narrow gap between his huge desk and the wall. He wore tight-fastening, waist-high trousers held up by braces, which he consistently *thwacked* against his pecs, as if to check they still worked.

The music from the main body of the building was barely audible in this little ventricle of business. Gov had dragged them through an elaborate, veiny pattern of back corridors and passages to reach his office, a place so far out of view that he could deny the conversation had ever happened.

'I didn't fight in a war—' Harry began.

'Why don't you shut up?' Sylvy spat.

'I didn't fight in a war, but my dad did,' Harry continued, icily calm. 'He told me all about it and I like to think of myself as a soldier sometimes. Respectable. Honourable.

What I'm trying to say is that we wouldn't want to cause trouble. We're well behaved. We wouldn't trash the place. If you let us stay, don't throw us out, then we'll blend in.' Harry paused, then lowered her voice. 'I can't say the same for the Sisters.'

'She's a bloody liar, she started the fight,' Sylvy shouted across the room. Harry, her voice quieter, cut through the small uproar.

'The Sisters will tip the place. Like those kids in Bradford that you read about in the paper, Gov.'

'Not if I throw them out now.' Gov went to stand but his legs got caught by the chair and his knees by the desk, trapped by his own furniture.

'The Sisters will tip it. I guarantee it. Tables, chairs, music stands, curtains, the lot. Who knows, maybe they'll use the piano strings as belts to keep their trousers up? I warn you, while the Sisters set foot in your hall, it's not safe. They're not honourable, respectable. They're not us. You should throw them out now. Or I don't know what will happen to it.'

'Enough!' Gov smacked his hand down on the desk.

'What do you mean, enough? I'm only talking. I can't guarantee that the Sisters aren't...'

'Stop!' Gov had to shout. His face was white and greasy.

'Let us have our say,' Char butted in. 'If you let these animals have it, you may as well throw it to the dogs.'

'What did you call us?' Leslie lunged at Char; Saint held her back.

'I won't have fighting in my hall. I've half a mind to let neither of you in here,' Gov said.

Char continued to plead with him, offering arguments, negotiations.

Meanwhile, a whisper from Tony brushed Harry's ear.

'I didn't know your dad fought in the war.'

'He didn't.' Harry stared straight ahead. 'He was five-foot-six, had asthma and wore glasses thick as a goldfish bowl.' Tony followed Harry's eyeline and saw the photos hanging about the room: Gov in the Home Guard; Gov next to his son in uniform; the son in uniform, dead-pose, alone, monumental; the medal from the pictured son's chest on the desk; a model Spitfire; a model Hurricane; various other bits of memorabilia, medals and trinkets from the war.

Gov burst.

'In the eyes of everyone who means anything in this world, this hall still belongs to me. Your talk about soldiers and war...' His brown eyes glistened like polished shoe leather. Mr George was in them. 'Why do you do this to yourself? We just got done with a war and as we're cleaning up the mess, you go and try to blow it up again. I fight to keep hold of what I've got, and what it's taken me years to get, what my son died for. I want to die having left something behind, and if that's not a child, then it's this pile of bricks.' He fingered a frame on the desk. 'Why would you want to unsettle everything for one minute in the spotlight? Kids like you don't last forever.' He looked at Harry, who steeled her gaze. 'It's time to be responsible and—'

'Do you hear that?' Tony interrupted. She turned towards the noise – or, as she soon realized, the lack of it. The music had stopped.

A scream cut the night. The slapping of little feet crescendoed towards the door. Petie flung it open, breathless, pale. A shock of red marred her white-blonde hair.

'Something happened...' she stuttered, looking at the faces, ragged breaths jacking up her chest. 'Something...'

'What?' Harry opened her arms wide. 'Petie, what?'

'They were one of yours!' Petie cried and lashed out towards Char. Harry intercepted, grabbing her collar and half-dragging her out of the office and down the corridor. The other Kings followed without thinking.

Gov tried to stand again but found himself imprisoned between the wall and the desk, stuck in the retreating scene. He might as well have been planted in the ground.

'That's it!' He reached for the phone. 'I'm calling the coppers.'

Another scream travelled through the dance hall. Petie's wails echoed down the corridors.

NINE

'I think she really likes me, but she's just scared to show it,' Cecil mused, as Al pretended to listen. 'She *wanted* to dance with me, but she's acting tough because it's what they all do, like Sylvy with her never-ending need to be uninterested. I'll get her back. I'll get them all back.'

He was standing in the gallery, leaning his chest against the railing, dangling his loosely crossed arms over the side – just like Marlon Brando straddles a motorbike, he thought. Rambling on with no audience but a distracted Al. The thin balcony was little more than a perch, providing a bird's-eye view of the hall and its movements. Cecil was watching the action from the circumference, one foot in, one foot out, waiting until the Sisters disappeared and the coast was clear for him to descend to the floor.

It wasn't that he needed Sylvy's permission to dance, or that he was afraid of her, or that he was afraid of Harry, or any of the other dancers or all the lights and the blare.

He had never been uncomfortable here before, so there was no reason for him to be uncomfortable now.

Still, ever since Harry had brushed him off outside the arcade, it seemed he could only mooch and think and smoke and drink. He hated the way he looked in the mirror, spent longer on his hair than ever before, and he visited the Grip-Teze this morning, alone, to play over and over again, just for the comfort of it, to know his hand could do something that wasn't pick at his own nails. He had been rejected by girls before, but the girls yesterday had dismissed him in a way that he found impossible to brush aside. Their sneers were imprinted on his mind, and he had come to Harfleur to be near them, to know that if he wanted it they would squirm under his hands.

The uncertainty was supposed to have ended tonight. He should have arrived at the dance floor and followed his hips to Harry, and she should have wilted against him. He should have taken her to the bar that he had chosen for them around the corner and sat her in the booth where the lamp was broken and he should have slid his right arm around her rear and his left between her legs and she should have had nothing the contrary to say about it. She should have kissed him back when he leaned in. She should have been his night – but she had left the dance floor with Sylvy, caught up in an evening all her own.

All those things he should have done remained unplayed. The music still spooled out down below, but none of it was his, none of it under his control. He couldn't return home; his father would ask him about his evening, about where he had been, who he had been with and why he wasn't with her still. He would talk about what he had done at Cecil's age, the women he had had and the places he had had them. Always two questions ahead, his father would ask how come his sister knew how to have fun, as if the pavement passed more easily under her feet. If only it was Sylvy that his father could drink with on the staircase. He had to make do with Cecil.

No doubt his father would mention what happened with Vernon – how he couldn't keep a hold of his pals. At one time, he and Vernon had been inseparable both day and night, talking the minutes out of hours, shooting breeze after breeze, sharing thoughts over shared sweets until their teeth were tender. He would practise conversation-starters when Vernon wasn't around and imagine his answers. They talked about women – to start with – before their conversations drifted towards cars and then to the stars above and the constellations inside of themselves and what made them shudder and groan and cry. Things he wouldn't admit to anyone else. Vernon was good for that, until Sylvy came along with her sharp glances and frank phrases that wrapped his friend around her finger. He became unavailable, too busy with the Coshers and the girls.

Cecil had tried to intervene with their world several times. What he wouldn't do to throw it off kilter. If Sylvy wanted to forget him, then he'd make sure she never did. Not letting her get what she wanted – that was a brother's job, right? A natural order had been upset with Sylvy's interruption, and Cecil only saw himself as setting it right. He had told lies about her to Vernon: that she had shared looks with other men on their street, that she wanted to bring down the Coshers from the inside and take the turf for herself. With every tale he spun, Cecil became more and more the boy who cried wolf, his word worth less and less until no one listened to him. Vernon cornered him and told him to stop trying to sabotage them or he would lose an eye. Cecil had reasoned with him, convinced that if he could make Vernon see that Sylvy was a poser, swaggering in her trousers, then things would return to normal. Two pals, like old times. Verne and Cecil.

'What's wrong with you, then, if she's not the problem?' Al asked, *humph*ing himself against the railings and shocking Cecil out of his thoughts. Al dove into his pocket, coming out with a fistful of tobacco, cheap cigarette skins and a lighter, busying himself with rolling.

'No one… nothing,' Cecil rushed out, before he thought about what he would say. He looked down at the dance floor and spied the tail end of the Kings leaving to speak with the owner. Al followed his gaze.

'I wouldn't get hung up on her. The blonde one's a swell bird. But the friend, the shorter one, she's...' Al searched for the right word. 'She's sort of wild, you know? Although I bet she'd be nice between the sheets, wouldn't she?' He nudged Cecil's elbow.

Cecil nodded half-heartedly.

'I'm not hung up. She's not that much of a catch.'

'What's *wrong*, then? You're making me miserable just looking at you.' Al nudged him again. He offered Cecil a cigarette, which he turned down. Shouts rose up from the dance floor as another song ended and the bodies sprinkled back towards the bar and the walls, resetting themselves in new combinations. Cecil wanted to be down there. It beckoned to him, and he watched, as a scientist looks through a microscope at the cells joining, repelling, mutating. He had no clue what he was doing here. He wondered whether, out of politeness to the universe, he should probably just leave.

'I said I don't know.'

Al perked up next to him.

'It must be *something*.'

It was on Cecil's tongue, nearly there on his lips.

'I don't know, I...' Fibonacci chatter, each sentence retracing its own step before taking another one forward.

The words tasted new, but familiar – waiting behind his closed lips for weeks. Perhaps he had already chewed them around in his mind before, practised them for the moment when someone asked because they wanted to know.

'Spit it out then,' Al urged.

From his split mouth and lapping eyes, it was clear what Al wanted to hear. He wanted Cecil to talk about a girl's legs and eyes and hair and waist. He didn't want to hear what Cecil wanted to say.

'It's just that... don't you sometimes feel a bit empty?'

Realization stole Al's face in less than a second.

'You mean...' Al gestured to his crotch. 'Sometimes. But that means you're not doing it with the right girl.'

'No, I mean... inside. Like you don't know what to do or...'

'I know what you mean. It comes with practice. I know that you've only done it once—'

'Twice,' on instinct, Cecil lurched in.

'—okay, twice. But there's a *knack* to it.'

Cecil hunched over the railings once more.

'That's not what I meant, I'm saying it all wrong. Are there times where you feel like you're a bit... *lost*.' He cringed as the word came out.

Al paused a moment, then laughed. He slapped the railing and the metal twang scorched at Cecil's insides. *Fool, fool, bloody fool*, he thought. If this ever got back

KELLY FROST

to the guys at the garage, Cecil shuddered, his life would be over.

'All the time,' Al responded. Cecil whipped his head round towards him. He was considering indulging in relief, when Al continued. 'Everybody knows that birds are a complete mystery, but getting lost and confused is half the fun, I suppose.'

'Well, I know that, but I just wanted to say—'

'The *secret*', Al continued in a conspiratorial whisper, 'is to pretend that you know what you're doing. In and out of the bed. And you've got to use all the lingo, too, pretend to know what you're talking about. She'll love it. Trust me.'

Cecil nodded, and gave up trying to explain. Was he speaking a different language to Al?

'Do you ever think about what we'll be doing in ten years? Twenty years?' Cecil tried a new line.

'What for?' Al asked.

'I don't know.'

'Well,' Al put some serious thought into it. 'I suppose I'll get married, have a couple of kids.'

'You want to?'

'I dunno, but it's... it's what you do, isn't it?' Al looked at him. 'I'll be in the same job, finishing work at half-past five, going home. All that.'

'Mm. All that.' Cecil thought of the garage, where he'd found himself working because his skinny arms (*chicken*

154

wings, his father called them) trembled under the weight of a labourer's load, and he'd passed out in the canning factory when it overheated last summer, sweat bright on his pale face. He considered how the grease would bake into the lines on his face as he got older, his back curved from bending over fenders.

'Is something wrong with that?'

'No.' Cecil was quick to shake his head.

Al, turning spiky: 'No, that's right. Sounds like a perfectly nice life to me.'

'Perfectly nice, just…'

'Just what?'

'Just can't believe that… the wife, kids, job. I guess you have to end somewhere once you start, don't you?'

'What are you on about?'

'Nothing.' Cecil waved his hand. Below them, the band switched tempo to a slick, quick beat and a mock-Elvis started singing 'Don't Be Cruel'.

'This song.' Al tugged on Cecil's jacket-sleeve, while mashing his finished cigarette into the floor. 'It's great. The American kids know a tune when they hear one. Plus, it makes the girls go…' he made a face, and Cecil laughed automatically. He supposed this was how it would be.

'Let's dance, then.' Cecil nudged Al towards the stairs while the others started to sing along to the words. The instinct to smash into Sylvy's world resurfaced as they descended from the stuffy rafters to the cooler altitudes of the dance floor, scuffed with the tappings of previous nights. If only Vernon was here, Cecil found himself thinking. He would know what to do. He would be someone to do it with.

Cecil kerplunked onto the floor like a lodestone, and ripples of his looks, his suit and hair, his cheekbones and dimples, went around the room. *The* size *of him,* one girl whispered, within earshot. The dance was not a ladies' choice, much to his relief. He scanned the room and saw a tight-busted honey-blonde. Her cheeks crumpled when she smiled; her eyes sparkled shallow blue. This kid wouldn't lead him on. As he idled towards her, she whispered to one of her friends and looked back at Cecil; they laughed. What were they saying about him? He brushed some dust off the forearm of his sleeve, from the railings, feeling paranoid. He checked his hair in the mirrors.

'So?' Al murmured from behind.

'So what?'

'Are you going after her? If you don't, I will.'

'In a minute, maybe,' Cecil replied.

'Too late, she's mine,' Al croaked a laugh and headed towards her, shoving his friend aside.

Cecil stepped backwards, towards the wall, bumping into someone. He apologized to the girl, a brunette.

'Would you like to dance?' she asked. He stumbled backwards at her forwardness.

'Um, no, I…'

'C'mon, I'm friendly.'

She grabbed his arm and pulled him into the melting pot of colours. Unwilling, but not unhappy, Cecil tried to make the most of it, aligning his limbs with the beat, trying to stick out his leg when his partner stuck out hers, twisting according to pattern, trying to fit and glide and swoop as prescribed. The partner reached a hand inside his collar and pressed hard against the back of his neck, her palm cold on his hot neck-skin. His stomach jumped while the music played on and he pulled away. The partner pulled back, thinking the move part of an elaborate dance, mistaking signs and signals for an improvised shimmy. The dance slipped into a kind of half-choreographed, drawing-board frenzy.

'I have to get a drink,' he shouted in her ear over the music. She let him go and sauntered off, tutting, knowing that he meant one drink and not two.

Trundling towards the bar, his attention swung all over the room. He spotted a group of kids in the centre of the floor, almost definitely Kings. A tall one, with white-blonde hair and a skinny frame, and the other two shorter, stumpier. They were playing with some poor boy. What would Vernon say, if he was stood next to him? *It's not right,* he might have mumbled. *Girls like that. Not the natural order of things.* Cecil's interest waned and he started to fixate on a dress shimmering scarlet in the dimly bright lighting.

When he turned back to the kids, a body was splayed on the floor, a red bloom spreading on its chest. Everybody seemed to be wearing red tonight. There was a scream.

A blood-wet knife skidded across the floor, almost colliding with Cecil's foot. Suits in grey, black and brown began running, almost off the bodies underneath them. A nearby girl covered her mouth to hush a scream. Others caught on, shouts and murmurs swelling to replace the music as 'Don't Be Cruel' dwindled into an embarrassed silence.

TEN

'I could get used to this.' Bernadette tried to catch her breath as the second ladies' excuse-me dance of the night ground to a halt. She was dizzy with the novelty of it all, her eyes glued to their reflections in the mirrors, which looked almost indistinguishable from the reflections of Kings.

'Is that the famous Cecil everyone talks about?' Nell pointed towards the gallery, her fingertip landing on a flimsy outline topped with a shine of ebony hair.

'Sylvy's brother, you mean?' Bernadette squinted to get a look.

'Eyes off,' Petie huffed. 'You know what they say about looking at the guys that aren't on Kings turf.'

'Oh, lay off.' Bernadette shook her head.

Nell leaned against the wall, gasping to regain lung capacity.

'I feel like my lungs are about to give out.'

'You know they've started saying that smoking gives you lung cancer—'

'That's just some stupid medical journal,' Nell interrupted Petie.

'You're only calling it stupid because you don't understand it!'

'Look there,' Bernadette nodded towards the door, silencing her squabbling friends. She had noticed the air stiffening between them. 'That's Drew, isn't it?'

They followed her gaze to see him trip over the lip of a doorframe, straighten and check his chestnut hair in the mirror.

'I didn't know he'd be here.' Nell started to walk towards him, but Petie grabbed her arm.

'Where do you think you're off to?'

'I'm going to say hello. Is that alright with you?'

'We need to stay here and keep an eye on things, like Harry said. We can't get distracted with boys.'

'I don't care what Harry said.' She shook off Petie's hand. 'I want to make a night of it. That's what I joined the Kings for. And my night is over there, on two legs, with a nice suit on, so will you let me go?'

'He'll come to you.' Bernadette smiled, as if there was something up her sleeve other than the balled-up handkerchief that her mother had embroidered with a *B*. 'We're Kings now, aren't we?' Drew spotted them and started to pick his way across the room. As he wandered over, bumping into dancers, apologizing, Petie mumbled:

'All we want is his lips and his body. If we could just, you know, take that and leave him, then that would be grand.' Nell and Bernadette had heard Harry say something similar before.

'Do you lot ever go anywhere separately?' Drew asked, approaching, from under his flop of unstyled hair, with that fidgety demeanour that reeked of shyness. At the school, boys used him as a football; he rarely made it to the end of the day without collecting another bruise.

'If these two ever leave me alone.' Petie stepped forward. Nell's face hardened; Bernadette hushed her with a pressured glance. *Who is she?* Nell mouthed, and it took Bernadette a moment to realize her friend was talking about Petie.

'The word on the street is that you're Kings now, or something,' Drew carried on. 'That was quick. You're not doing anything stupid though, right? I'm not going to see you in the papers, am I?' No one answered.

'Let's get to it.' Petie rubbed her hands together. 'I promised Nell one kiss, and I don't see why you two can't go ahead for a dance and get this over with. Obviously, she's not capable of asking for herself.'

161

'I just got here, Petie, and besides—'

'Besides what?' Petie clipped. She balled the air into her fingers with a tight fist, a flash of violent speech that had her friends sharing glances.

'I had no idea you were such a *spiv*,' Drew grimaced. In the mirrors, Nell saw Petie's eye glint off the room; she recognized a look on her face that she'd seen on Harry's. She saw Petie dare not to change it.

'Who are you calling a bloody spiv? I've been a King two days and you're writing me off like the rest of them.'

'Rest of who, Petie? No one tunes in to what's happening with your Kings.'

'I don't see what your problem is,' Petie spat. 'I know you'd hang around with the Hackers if they let you in, measly Drew. Just kiss Nell and this will be over, and we can move on to more pressing matters, like what I'm going to request from the band.' Her hand flirted with the cuff of Drew's jacket.

'You can't rent me out to your friends—'

'Oh, I didn't realize you'd gone all uptight, Drew. It was a bit different last week at the council hall when you promised a kiss to Nell and gave it to me—'

'Because you told me Nell wasn't interested anymore!' Drew said. Petie grabbed his wrist and kept her skinny fingers encircled around it like a watchstrap.

Nell's eyes began to burn.

'Drew's talking nonsense,' Petie scoffed. 'He doesn't remember what happened.'

'Let's not fight over him,' Bernadette eased in. 'It's not worth our time. Let's carry on dancing. Look, the band is playing Elvis!' A wannabe crooner gripped the microphone in both hands and attempted Elvis's 'Don't Be Cruel'.

Petie thrust Drew towards Nell. Nell pushed him back, trying to spin the conflict into a game; the trick usually worked. Bernadette stepped into the middle and held him still. From a distance, the scene was comical.

It was easy for them to miss the three girls who approached from behind. Taller and wearing black suits, they looked like the long, late-afternoon shadows of Petie, Nell and Bernadette. Their hair was overdone, flopping onto their faces, and their collars pulled up cheekbone-high.

Drew cleared his throat, alerting the kids to the new presence. Upon noticing them, Petie took a step back, instinctually dissociating herself from any childish behaviour displayed by the others. Bernadette inspected all three, noting that the tallest one stood lightly on her left foot, limping slightly. She recognized her from the streets – that same loose energy sparking in her fingers, and a familiar, pale face – but she couldn't say which side of the Bridge she knew her from.

'You're Kings, aren't you?' one of them – the girl with the limp – said, sneering.

'Looks like they'll let any runts do their dirty work these days, huh?' The second, with acne scars embedded deep in her cheeks, shot off.

'Who are you calling runts?' Petie moved forward to stand face to face with the confronters. 'Who *are* you?'

'Must be Seven Sisters…' Nell filled in.

'It figures, with those cheap suits…' Petie muttered. Bernadette pawed at her elbow, trying to pull her back from the brink of a situation with a sharp drop.

'Harfleur's not your hall,' the limping girl asserted.

'It *will* be after tonight. You'd better start looking for another place to dance.'

'You're on Seven Sisters turf, and you've insulted one of us, to make matters worse… if I say leave, *leave*.'

'It's *our* hall.' Petie threw out her breast, trying to add centimetres to her height.

'Say that one more time and—' the acne-scarred girl began, but her words got stuck somewhere before her lips.

Petie, laughing, grabbed Drew – who was slowly turning towards the swirling milieu of dancers to become just another set of trouser legs – and pulled him close, clamping their lips into a wet kiss. Elvis's copy screamed a note off-key. A chorus of *hey*s and *oi*s from the Kings trio and the Seven Sisters crumpled into each other. Noise creamed into thick happening and the kids notched towards violence. Drew set himself free and scrambled off across the hall, wiping his mouth.

The girl with the limp swiped a flick knife from her sleeve. Petie checked her back pocket and found nothing. She elbowed Nell, who replied by showing her a pair of empty hands. Their three confronters smiled, thinking the tension was over. Civility would resume, the song would finish, and another would play. The night's clockwork carnival would close its doors on time, and everything would proceed as usual.

But another flick cut through the buff hall noise, and their heads turned to Bernadette, who gripped a little blade. Beads of sweat from the heat of the dance hall, the last dance catching up to her, shone on her forehead. Her breaths still refused to add up nicely.

'I thought bringing a blade was what you were supposed to do!' Bernadette panic-whispered. Petie and Nell replied with clueless eyes. None of them knew *what* procedure was, or whether there was one. Especially not now.

'Are you going to use it though, kid?' the acne-scarred girl asked.

'I'll put it right through you,' Bernadette exploded. 'Back up! Go on!' Like a child, she thought, shooing pigeons.

A dancer bumped into Bernadette's back, shunting her forwards into the limping girl, who pushed her to the ground. The knife flailed from the end of Bernadette's arm. Petie followed the blade with her eyes, flashing jewellery-reflections from nearby dancers – none of whom had cottoned on to the scuffle. Nell helped Bernadette up: the three of them stood, as always, in formation.

The limping girl jabbed the air. She grinned as Nell and Petie backed up slightly, unarmed, uncertain. Bernadette stood, still holding the sad blade, waiting for a distraction: it would be humiliating to put the blade away now, but she was unsure what was expected of her. At this point in the pictures, the fight would continue into fluid choreography, or the camera would cut away from the groaning man bleeding onto the pier.

The song crescendoed to its final chorus. Another dancer hit Bernadette's back, as the limping girl lost balance on her weak ankle and tripped forwards. She jammed her knife, hard.

Bernadette grimaced and fell forwards, embracing her assailant in a slumped hug. The two bodies, fitted snugly together, could have been slow dancers caught out in a fast beat, either too early or too late for the doo-wop. Soon though, the taller girl moved back and let the body crumple, looking down at the red-sheen blade in her hand.

'Wipe the handle and slide it!' her friend hissed, wide-eyed. She stood, immobile, staring at the blade, until one of the others snatched the knife, scrubbed at its handle with her sleeve and slid the little metal shard across the floor and out of sight. It passed under a hundred stamping feet. With some yanking, some looks at each other, the three suits retreated into the dance menagerie.

Petie bent to the ground, trying to press down on the shirt-staining mess spreading across Bernadette's chest. She brushed a hand through her own hair, streaking the white-blonde with red – accidental warpaint.

A girl, no older than thirteen, boogied into their clearing to plug the gap. Her foot collided with the body and she turned to see what was on the floor. She paused in horror, hand clapped over her mouth. Her scream pierced the air.

The music continued jauntily: *Don't be cruel... To a heart that's true... Don't be cruel...*

ELEVEN

Nell kneeled, her face clattering with tears. She was poised like a gardener over a wilted flowerbed, winter frost damning its growth. Dancers clomped and thrummed around her, people moving erratically towards the cloak-room, the exit, some nearer to Nell, while the music petered out in the background.

Harry stood at the mouth of the corridor and watched on as the hall tried to continue its dance, curdling out of tune while teenagers got the hell out of there. Her eyes were magnetized to the body, so limp and lean on the floor. Thoughts accelerated through her mind as she tested herself for liability: if she hadn't asked the kid to be a King, would she be bleeding out on the parquet? If she hadn't brought the kids here tonight, would one of them be bleeding out on the parquet? If there had been no parquet, would the kid have been here to bleed out on it?

168

A hand was pulling on her shoulder: Tony, dragging her away from the scene.

'We should run,' she said, softly, not letting up her grip on Harry's shoulder. 'We can't be here when the coppers arrive. We can't be anywhere near it.'

'The kids... we can't leave them,' Harry murmured, pushing inwards. Tony, after the blank air started to grow between them, followed, elbowing dancers out of her way. When they reached the little group, Nell whipped up her head. Her breath blustered their faces; she drew them in uneven rags, their stirrings beating and confusing the air. Saint dripped in from behind, holding up Petie by the arm like a limp ragdoll.

'Look what they did,' Petie wept, unbounded.

'You.' Harry pointed to Nell. She couldn't remember her name. 'Who did it? Was it Sisters?'

'Who *else* would it be?' Petie blubbered.

'I don't know...' Nell trailed.

'Well, what did they say?' Harry asked. 'What did you say to *them*?'

'You think it's *our* fault this happened?' Nell cried.

Tony continued dragging on her shoulder, trying to yank her away.

A microphone *twanged* as it had done in the ladies' excuse-me dance. This time, the announcer kindly, panickedly, requested the dancers to leave the hall as

169

soon as possible while the management dealt with an *incident*.

'They *looked* like Sisters,' Nell went on. 'But I can't know for sure...' She stared down at Bernadette – or what was Bernadette.

'We need to *run*, Harry.' Saint tugged on her sleeve.

'That's what I said,' Tony added.

'Shut it, *both* of you.' Harry batted away Tony's hand. 'Kings don't *run*.'

'Kings don't get kids *killed*.' Tony pointed at the motionless body on the ground. Something bit in her throat and she jerked her head away.

'Tony, you know this had nothing to do with us,' Harry reasoned, quietly.

'You want to tell yourself that so you can sleep tonight?' Tony asked. 'That you—'

'Harry,' Jackie cut in, eyes bulbed up to her. All the Kings were looking up at her, Harry soon realized – perhaps so they didn't have to look at the dead girl near their feet. They were in their worst nightmares, and Harry was the one to guide them out, one way or another. She felt it settle on her shoulders.

Across the hall, Sylvy, Char, the other Sisters had poured out of the corridor onto the dance floor – and now, seeing the body, they were retreating. There were still thickets of dancers around them as Harry plunged through, jostling a path, with Kings on her heels. Sylvy saw her advancing and yanked open the fire-exit door, ushering Sisters through before throwing herself out of it.

Harry caught the door before it shut behind them and burst into the alley.

'You did this,' she raged, her fingertip close to Sylvy's nose. Harry had her backed against the wall of the side street, hand scrunched in the shoulder of her jacket.

'It wasn't us,' Sylvy replied; her defensiveness was strained, pleading. 'It could have been anyone. Harry, this was some idiot with a knife, not us. We need to disappear to keep from *all* of us disappearing down a hole—'

'There's no *us*.' Still pinned against the brick. '*That* in there...' she pointed back to the door, Kings and fleeing dancers streaming out, '*that* has to be paid for.' A girl lay dead on the floor – there had to be consequences.

'With what? You want someone else to die? Is that what would make you happy?' Sylvy gave a hoarse half-laugh.

'Andover Patch. Tomorrow, it's got our name on it, because it's where we're going to fight for the turf. Once and for all.'

'Harry—' Char tried to butt in.

'A fight, tomorrow. An eye for an eye, you know how it goes.'

'Look, we'd be happy to call it a truce now.' Sylvy stuck out her hand for a shake, itching to escape. Sirens grew and Kings and Sisters alike swivelled their heads towards the noise. Harry looked down at the hand in repulsion.

'Please, take it,' Saint whispered from behind.

'She's right,' Sylvy nodded at Saint. 'We can talk turf later. Take the hand.'

'There's not a cat in hell's chance I'm taking that hand.' Harry started shaking her head, without even a pause, walking backwards and letting Sylvy go. 'Six o'clock, tomorrow, at the Patch.'

Sylvy looked at her, wide-eyed. There was nothing she could do to stop Harry now that Edie, and the Kings, had set her going. The nasal drone of police sirens wailed louder on the main road, near the front entrance. Both gangs tracked the headlights skimming the brick wall, flashing over their faces. Sylvy nodded. The battle lines had been drawn.

The Sisters slunk into the night. Harry watched them melt, before murmuring to her Kings:

'We need to go.'

'That's what I've been saying, you never *fucking* listen to me.' Tony set her mouth. Saint, Harry could tell, was unsure what to do with hers.

'Where's Petie?' she asked. Jackie pointed towards the doorway, where Nell was whining questions.

'But what about Bernie?' Nell opened her bloody hands to Harry as the leader approached.

'Bernie's dead.' Petie shook her. 'Someone will call someone, and someone will clean it up. You want to answer to the coppers?' Nell tried to mumble something but no words came out.

'Come on.' Harry ushered them towards the shadowed end of the alley, where Kings were climbing over a wire fence. 'We need to lay low somewhere.'

Petie started out behind them, one hand on the fence. Nell stayed put, glancing backwards.

'Nell, come on. What are you doing?' Petie asked, fixing to follow the Kings. She tugged at her friend's arm. 'Don't you want to come?'

'No, I want to stay here with Bernie.'

'Come on! Don't you want to be a *King*?' she hissed.

Nell, her eyes wide, simply replied:

'No… no, I don't think I do.'

'We don't have time for this.' Harry shoved the two down the side street.

Harry was the last of the Kings to leave the alley, as she had been the last to enter the hall. The slow toiling sirens of the law – now directly outside the front entrance – mixed with the stale whispers of spilled-out teenagers.

Police blasted into the hall, their panicked footsteps rushing around, their swivelheads noticing the absence of perpetrators. Gov stood with them, gupping like a fish and pawing the little hair remaining on his head. Nothing was left in the hall but reckless kids growing up the mirrors like vines, clinging to their own reflections. The Kings and the Seven Sisters had vanished, the only trace of them exhaled cigarette smoke, wafting and cuddling the air.

TWELVE

Sylvy should have gone home. With blood on her mind, she should have called it a night; she should have followed Cecil and tracked the gaps between streetlamps to their flat, where she should have sat under the windowsill, ears cracked open for the sirens, and written to Vernon. In that letter, she should have put down what happened in the dance hall while it was still fresh and pulsing in her fingers, and apologized to him for her carelessness in letting it go so far.

Instead, she was in Pichetti's, trying not to look Louisa Gray in the eye. It was difficult, since there wasn't much else to look at in the twenty-four-hour Italian–English café: wood-panelling that oozed decades of fried-egg stench, an offers board above the untended counter where a lazy hand had chalked prices, mallow light dousing yellow tablecloths, small shabby tables. There were only four girls in the room – including Char standing beside her, fluttering, eyes fixed ahead and twisting her rings as if trying to take the fingers off with them.

Ouisa was waiting for her to start talking, but now that Sylvy was here, adrenaline washing up against the backs of her eyeballs, the reason for coming had drained away. It must have fallen onto the pavement somewhere between Pichetti's and the back of the dance hall where Ouisa's sullen face had first appeared in her mind. It felt like hours since then, but the wall clock told her it was half-past eleven. Nights never ended when death was in them, Sylvy was beginning to suspect.

As Sisters had dribbled off to their domestic corners and found places to wait out the night, Sylvy had launched into planning the next step: how the Sisters would win tomorrow's battle. But winning the war, she soon realized, was more important. A battle here, a battle there, it meant nothing and would never end; it was like spitting on a plant and expecting it to flourish. The Seven Sisters needed to become more than the Coshers' leftovers, scrapping over what remained of their turf. The gang needed to make a name for itself to become respected, to become feared. Officials needed to let them through for the Sisters to last. With Ouisa on the table, it was all to play for.

A siren came loose from the night's tapestry outside. Sylvy turned her back to the glass front, which busked a weak, rosin-yellow light onto the damp road.

'That something to do with you?' Ouisa remarked, faintly amused. She was sat sideways in a booth, legs up on the scuffed-leather seat with her back against the wall. Smoke trailed around her and Roz, the girl who sat on the opposite booth. A butt-filled ashtray and a half-played game of cards waited for their attention on the table.

Everyone knew that Ouisa hung out at Pichetti's. It was the only thing you could count on about her. As unpredictable as the length of a piece of string, Ouisa had a spooling reputation that started with punching a vicar and getting away with it – and pretty much ended there, too. It couldn't get much better than that. Sylvy had once overheard Ouisa telling the story from the other side of a milk bar. She had been in the church hall for a council-run dance when the black-haired vicar had thanked everyone for coming; he felt it was the Lord's will to give back to those who have all suffered terribly. Ouisa didn't much like that and pushed the vicar into the punch bowl where the purple drink stained his face the same colour as the shiny black eye she gave him. From there, the rumour swelled that talking to Ouisa was like walking on a lion's back, a shortcut to becoming her breakfast. You could never say the right thing. There was too much tetch in that girl. The pattern of fear around her. No wonder the Sisters had splintered off when Sylvy announced that Ouisa was her next stop of the night.

Escaping the vicar's wrath had nothing to do with his talent for forgiveness and everything to do with Ouisa's father, who was a senior policeman about as crooked as his own rancid teeth. To make matters even better for Ouisa, Sergeant Gray was brothers with a councillor twice as crooked as he was. With connections like those, it was no wonder that Edie had scooped her up into the Kings. For reasons unknown, Ouisa fell out with them after a few months and started to date a Cosh Boy for a while. Before long, she graduated to the big leagues, washing money for East End gangs out the back of family-run cafés that were running close to the red line – cafés like Pichetti's.

'What's wrong with her?' Ouisa nodded at Char, who was swaying slightly on her feet. Ouisa had not invited them to sit. 'She's not going to fall over, is she?'

'She'll be fine.' Sylvy glanced at Char. 'Won't you, Char?'

'Get on with it, then.'

'I'm Sylvy—'

'And I care because…' Ouisa picked up one of the cards on the table, looking for somewhere to put it down.

'Because I'd like to propose a partnership with you.'

Ouisa's hand froze, the card still in it.

'I don't do partnerships.' Sylvy flicked her eyes pointedly at Roz. Ouisa huffed. 'Roz isn't a partner. She can play cards like the devil.'

Ouisa brushed at the rough curls around her ears and pushed a pair of thick, black-plastic glasses up her nose. Sylvy spied small metal boxes fixed behind her ears; hearing aids secreted in the arms of the frame – the newest technology, the newest fashion. A bomb had blasted away her eardrums and she had spent three years trapped in a hollow of silence before the country's technology caught up to its children. Sylvy had always assumed that she wore the glasses to hide her deafness – *no one likes to admit they don't hear as well as the next man,* one of the Sisters had once remarked when Ouisa's name came up. Standing there, Sylvy wondered whether there was another reason.

'The Seven Sisters are looking to branch out,' Sylvy pressed on, kicked by the shock still running through her system.

'Sylv…' Char tried to enter the conversation, her voice wavering.

'Where do I know the name Seven Sisters from?' Ouisa waved the card around in her hand. Roz tapped her finger on the table, irritated that the fate of the game was on a hinge. With a slight grin at Ouisa, Sylvy understood: she had to earn her inclusion in the conversation. Her time didn't come for free.

'Ah, that's right,' Ouisa said. 'You're what the Coshers left behind.'

'More than that.' Sylvy stepped forward, removing the trembling Char from her periphery.

'Is that so?'

'We'd like to make it to the surface.'

'Speak in plain language.'

'Fight with us, tomorrow. Join us and our side.'

Ouisa put down the card, finally. Sylvy was playing the game now. No more faffing. This felt good; she was good at this. If only Vernon could see her now.

'And why would I do that?'

'We're fighting the Kings.'

'Alright, I'm interested.'

'And you hate the Kings.'

'Don't tell me what I do and don't hate.'

'Sorry.'

'Don't give me sorries.'

Sylvy went mute. Ouisa leaned back, flexing her arm over the booth's backrest.

'The first question is what you want to get out of this partnership, because I don't think it's just another body on the pitch, is it?' Sylvy shook her head. 'Feel free to use words, if you'd like. Or don't.'

'We want to talk to your dad, and your uncle. You know, we're a serious gang, looking to expand our turf and what we do on that turf. We're going to need protection, and in return I'm sure we could give them a commission.'

'The fact you're telling me you're a serious gang makes you sound like a chicken that's strutting around pretending to be a peacock.'

'I thought you'd understand.'

'And why is that?'

'Because, you know…'

'Because I'm not a guy? Oh please', she shook her head, 'that stopped mattering long ago. That's how I got here. By acting like one of them. Shame on you for thinking we're different, that we need *special*—'

'I didn't mean—'

'Oi, don't fucking interrupt me!' Ouisa launched out of the booth, her finger in Sylvy's face. She cooled off, walking to the counter to fetch a bottle half-full of whisky and bringing it back to the table. 'You're expecting me to jump at this honour? That just because I can help, I will. What can you do for me?'

'What?' Char blurted. Sylvy gave her a look: *shut it*.

'You didn't seriously think you could walk in here and ask me to fight with you and give you a leg up and offer nothing in return. So, what's on the table, then? Because there better be something.'

'You get some of the best nights of your life. You get sisters.'

Ouisa clunked the bottle on the table. Reddish anger poured into her cheeks.

'Aw, that's very sweet. But that's not how it works. You want to climb up in the world, put your foot on the rung of this greasy ladder, you've got to prove it. Dad doesn't do handouts, neither do I.'

'What do you want, then?' Sylvy reasoned.

'A favour.'

'What is it?' Char tested, fear bubbling in her voice.

'I need something delivered to Tottenham Court Road, tonight. You do that for me, I'll consider your offer.'

'No, we can't,' Char murmured.

'Char, damn it, be quiet!' Sylvy snapped behind her; there was too much energy lashing in her limbs. She turned back to Ouisa, slowing her voice. 'Don't listen to her, we could do it. We *can* do it.'

'I thought she was your leader.' Ouisa cocked her head.

'She's just… frazzled.'

'We can't do it, Sylv.'

'We *can*,' Sylvy talked over her.

'Not after tonight. We can't, not tonight.'

'What happened tonight?' Ouisa asked.

'Nothing happened tonight, it's fine.' Sylvy raised her hand to Ouisa, before turning to deal with Char.

'It's not fine!' Char started to raise her voice. 'A little girl died.'

Ouisa stood. Roz surveyed the cards silently.

'I'm telling you, she's fine, she's right as rain.'

'She doesn't bloody look it.'

'Look, she's fine, okay?'

'Not tonight, we can't,' Char continued to repeat.

Ouisa, pressing closer, murmured at Sylvy: 'Get out. Come back to me when you've stopped crying over spilled milk. You won't last five minutes—'

'Spilled blood.' Char strained against Sylvy's hands, wanting to lash out at Ouisa.

'I mean it, get out of this café or you won't see another,' Ouisa burned. Sylvy, apologizing, led Char out onto the street. Ouisa returned to her cards with Roz, shaking her head.

'Sylv!' Char called as Sylvy strode ahead, hair jockeying on her shoulders. 'Wait for me, will you? Look, I'm sorry.'

Once she had rounded the corner, away from Pichetti's, Sylvy came to an abrupt stop and turned to confront Char.

'What was that all about?' Her voice bounced off the nearby houses, and she lowered it. 'We've lost the hall, Harry's called a fight. And now, we've burned our bridges with Ouisa. Tonight's turned into a mess.'

'And you're forgetting that someone *died*.' Char's eyes filled – Sylvy turned away from her.

'Of course I didn't forget. But we didn't do the killing.' Sylvy steeled her look.

'Then who was it?'

'I don't know. But we'll find out, I sent the others to find out. There were three of them. No one got a good look. I wouldn't put it past Harry to have bribed them to push us into all-out war. After what we did at the football match last week.'

'After what *you* did,' Char said. 'I know you can't help it but, Sylvy, why?' Both went quiet for a moment. Sirens tore another hole in the night.

'C'mon,' Sylvy mumbled, and continued on and away from the main streets, plunging into alleys. In her haste, she bumped into a woman with a trench coat done up to her cheekbones; she didn't apologize.

'We can still get out of this fight,' Char mused from behind.

'Why would we want to get out of it?' Sylvy pressed on. 'We promised the boys not to lose the turf. It was ours to keep, and we can keep it if we fight the Kings for it. Which we're going to have to do.' Footsteps had dried up behind her, she realized. Char had stopped several paces back, and Sylvy wandered over to her.

Char whispered: 'We both know that this has nothing to do with the boys anymore. It hasn't for a while.'

'Oh, piss off!' Sylvy shook her head.

'Stop using them as an excuse to—'

'Leave it alone.' Sylvy went to punch the brick wall, but

drew back her fist. It was still bruised from the last time. 'Pull yourself together, Char. What happened in there was… embarrassing.'

'We told ourselves, when the Sisters started to act as we do now, that we'd never say that. *Pull yourself together*,' she mimicked Sylvy.

'Yeah, well it's not the same now, is it? Not after tonight.'

'Exactly.' Char lifted her head, locking eyes with Sylvy. 'It's got ugly, what we started. It was a stab at being different, escape from all that other stuff, hang out with the boys, be like them. But it went wrong somewhere.' She paused. The alley lagged around them. 'It makes me wish I'd never known you.'

Harshly, Sylvy spat: 'If you had never known me, you'd be nothing. You'd still be waiting on that doorstep where I found you, trying not to cry. Do you remember? Charlie, Charlie, the boys were making fun of you.'

'Of course I remember,' she scoffed. This was the favour Char could never repay: a sister, a distraction; a reality unrecognizable from the one she had always known. Sylvy made gangtime a holiday that never ended. 'I just don't want to see you get hurt, Sylvy. I don't want to see any of them get hurt.' Her tight pout crimped and she dug the heels of her hands into her eye sockets, grinding out tears. 'I'm sorry about Ouisa, I'm sorry about all of it.'

Sylvy softened. Her anger waned, and empathy trod in. She rushed forwards, as if to catch Char from falling into a puddle, and embraced her, wiping the warm tears from cheeks she knew well.

'I should take over,' Sylvy breathed. 'You don't want to fight, I get it. But if Harry's insisting on one, then we've got to win it, or there's no Sisters anymore.'

'You need a fight to prove you've got a fist at all.' Char smiled weakly. 'Alright. It won't be long before the Sisters work out that I won't throw a punch anyway. Not since...'

'I know, you don't have to say it. If you like, you don't even have to be there, at the Patch. I can make an excuse.'

'Don't be daft. I'll be there. But if we win tomorrow, promise me that it will go back to the way it was, as normal as it can be until the boys are back. No more dead kids in dance halls, no one getting stuck with blades, not on Seven Sisters Road.'

'You know I can't promise that,' Sylvy replied.

'I *am* sorry, about Ouisa—'

'Forget about her,' Sylvy cut her off, smiling tightly. 'No matter what we wanted from her, Ouisa probably would have told us to get out. She wished she was one of the Sisters.'

'Our Sisters.'

'That's right.'

Tears welled in Char's eyes again, and she apologized. Sylvy told her to stop apologizing.

'Can you let the others know that you're in charge now? That the fight is on?' Char asked. 'I don't think I can face anyone right now.' Sylvy slung her arm around Char's shoulders as they walked step in step towards home.

'Of course, Char.'

THIRTEEN

The Kings Head was closed. The Crone had suffered a relatively busy night, the place crammed with all manner of life from dates to elderlies to tourists to kids pushing their luck, each with something to tell, something to swindle. She had stood behind the bar for seven hours, a solitary sentinel, watching the clock thrum through the minutes, and dwelling on the traces of the late husband that had left her with this pile of bricks: the paint colours they had picked together, the choice of brews, the arrangement of the chairs and tables in little clusters, even the missing apostrophe between the *g* and the *s* in The Kings Head. On the day that it fell from the wall, a *dink* and *clatter* into the road, she watched as her husband picked it up, tossed it around in his hands and swept back inside only to start beating her over the head with it. When he died two years later, from what others called a tragic heart attack, leaving his will open, unfinished and disputable – and his relatives unbothered – she had never replaced the apostrophe. It sat under the bar, where she kept the spare napkins.

At eleven o'clock, the final few rumblers and drunksters – but none, thank God, too drunk to handle – had stumbled out. The Crone stood on the doorstep and watched them leave. She took a moment to look up, left, right, as if checking her neck could still swivel, her eyes could still look, noticing the shops that had closed since last week, the ruins slowly piecing themselves back into buildings, the cars lined up and sleeping, performing this nightly checklist for herself. She had heard a distant kerfuffle, a squint of sirens, and thought nothing of it, ignoring fury, and returned inside – where she had swiped the bar clean of peanut crumbs and beer spillages, switched off the lights. She had moved upstairs, ready to resign for the night, removing dentures, one final evening smoke.

Before long, a group began tearing her night into scraps of yelling and laughter. They called to her from the street – *let us in, let us in, old Crone* – and she tottered to the window, irritated, and lifted it just enough to pop out her head. Kings.

'I just put my head on the pillow!' she shouted down. The Kings stood on the kerb, begging her to let them in.

'Then get in there and pick it back up again!' Harry hollered. The Crone drew inwards, looking longingly at her pillow and its head dent.

'Are you in trouble?' she asked, leaning back out.

'Always!' Harry chirped – but her smile faltered. The Crone sensed a tired rehearsedness to Harry's cheek; something raw and fresh poking through that confidence. A strange protectiveness came over her. Rolling her eyes – not without affection – the Crone retreated inside, shoving her legs into some trousers and walking them downstairs, snatching the keys off the hook in the hallway. Sleepy and dutiful, she emerged at street level to their cheers, and held open the door for them to enter.

The Kings filed in, taking their rightful places among the tatty velvet seats.

'Where's your twin?' the Crone mumbled to Jackie.

'Long night, she couldn't stay awake. I'll give her the report tomorrow morning.' What Jackie had meant to say was that Leslie hadn't been able to control her shivering. Around the side of Harfleur, both of them had snuck twin-words to each other under their breaths as the leaders made plans for a fight, lacing their fingers in each other's hands for comfort. They decided that one had to stay, but neither could stop thinking about the dead girl on the parquet. Tony had gone missing, too, in their scramble out of Harfleur Hall. Drifting off to a bar, they assumed.

'What's wrong with you lot?'

The Crone tried to get the story out of them. The clock ticked past midnight into the hours of trouble.

'I'd appreciate it,' Harry whispered near the Crone's ear, 'if you'd leave us be, for now. A bit of a shock this evening, you see.' The Crone *hmm*ed, letting the door shut behind Harry. She moved towards the back, shuffling about, taking upturned chairs off tables and setting them in neat alignments, switching the lights on with a *buzz*.

'If we keep this routine up with the Sisters, I suppose I'll never sleep,' Harry chewed the thought with her mouth open. She leaned over the bar, grabbing a pint glass and a bottle of whisky. At the rise of the bottle, the Crone nodded her permission, and she unhitched the cap and poured a shot into the pint glass, downing it in one swift movement.

'You're not going to drink a pint of whisky, are you, Harry?' Saint prodded, a loose laugh on her lips. Harry replied by pouring another shot and throwing it back with a hard, unforgiving stare. 'Look, Harry, I really think...'

'I know you do, Saint Joan. That's all you ever do.' The response was quick and cutting. Blush in her cheeks, Saint settled on a bar-stool and produced a pencil from a fold somewhere and a slim packet of cigarette papers from her pocket. She poised to write.

'Right, what are we looking at?'

Harry reached over, took the pencil from Saint's hand and rolled it across the bar, out of reach.

'How about we enjoy what's left of the night, huh?' Harry sighed. 'It could be our last in this pub, taking our name from that sign, if the Sisters have anything to say about it.' Harry looked out the window, as if spotting a curl of future around the corner.

'Don't say that,' Jackie begged. She lit a cigarette and began leisurely smoking, as if to plump the surroundings.

Without the pencil, Saint rubbed her fingertips together, twitching. She restrained herself from grabbing it. Her eyes scanned the room for a way to occupy them and started to line up the salt cellars in a neat row. The sum of Saint's enjoyment, Harry knew, existed in the pencil notes on cigarette papers, lined-up salt cellars; plans and rules and lines and neat divisions. The wobbly lines of tonight, its blurred moral edges, were making her feel nauseous. Harry could see it; she stoked it, in the mood for cruelty. She could do without Saint's righteousness for a minute.

'Harry, don't be ridiculous,' Saint murmured.

'*Don't be ridiculous*,' Harry mocked back.

'I mean it.'

'Yeah, I bet you do.'

'You're not saying anything, Harry. What happened tonight really puts us in jeopardy.'

'Saint, you could stop making it so bleeding obvious that you know more words than I do.'

'This isn't a *game*.'

'Oh, don't we know that. But it is yours, Miss Joan. Your chance to play rough. It's gotten a bit too rough now, hasn't it? Well, there's the door.' Harry thrust her arm towards the pub's entrance. She remembered when Saint had first walked through it, hair awry, seeking shelter. Huffing lobs of breath over her lips as she ducked in the nearest pub and hid behind one of the velvet curtains, fresh tears springing. She had squeezed her eyes shut, like forcing herself into a dream, as a chatter of guys walked past the windows, hounding someone who had disappeared from their streets and into another world. Edie had been there; she asked Saint if the Kings should go after them. Saint declined. *I could never* – their introductions to Saint's posh stylings. A shaking kid who glued them together with her thirst for organization. The Kings had taught her how to unwind, and were still training Saint Joan to snap when she needed to. Harry had always assumed there would come a time when she left, a visitor grown bored with their dustbowl entertainment.

'I'm not leaving.' Saint was firm, as if reading Harry's mind. 'I'm a King.'

'Sure, I believe you, love.' Harry refused to look her in the eye. 'I also remember Edie telling me that you were nice to have around and all that, but, well…'

'Go on, Harry, you might as well say it. You're halfway there.'

'You don't really need to hang around with us lot, when all is said and done. Kids like you weren't what Edie had in mind when she started the Kings.' Saint shook her head, in disbelief that Harry could be so wrong. 'Admit it, you could leave any second now and walk into another life, a nicer one, probably.' Saint scoffed. Harry pressed on. 'A King would hit me right now.'

'You want me to hit you, don't you, Harry?' Rare stand-offishness rose up in Saint. 'Would that make you feel better? Tony would, but where is she? You've pissed her off too. You'll be left alone soon if you're not careful, Harry. You and your war to keep the Kings on top, to keep them together... not exactly working out, is it?'

'Saint, stop it,' Jackie piped up from behind.

'I don't know who you are anymore, Harry. Since the summer, you're all *wrong*. You talk about wanting to stay on the streets forever, but it's like you want to disappear instead.' Saint resumed lining up the salt cellars.

Harry slammed her hands down on the table, shocking the others. She was depleted, raging – and mumbled *I need a minute*. She wandered towards the back room of the pub, where the payphone and the little curtained doorway led off to a half-landscaped pub garden with scattered picnic tables, ashtrays, leaning umbrellas. In the nook of privacy

near the back door, Harry scrabbled for the string con-
nected to a bare bulb and pulled it with trembling fingers
for light. She inspected the telephone book, adverts clam-
bering up and down a corkboard, the plastered segments
from *Motoring Weekly* with cars for sale, televisions for
sale, women for sale.

Her chest began to rise and fall, rise and fall, her
ribcage lurching and trying to rip out of the skin.
Heartbeats clanged in her ears, in her mouth, in her eyes,
and she breathed and breathed and breathed but it wasn't
enough; air kept passing through her like a tunnel and her
funnel onto the adverts went skewed and she leaned over,
grabbing at her chest, trying to rip something off, tear
something away, to no avail. Pulling down her collar, she
let the skin breathe and dry off in the sunny space outside
eyes. She allowed herself the terrifying luxury of panic.
She thought of Mr George, of Bernadette, of the brawl-
to-be, of death and of time and of money and of war. She
had let Mr George down. She couldn't let Edie down. Or
the Kings – *her* Kings – either. How would she convince
them to fight? Would the scared ones need an option to
leave? Could she offer them that? And fighting – why had
she done that, pushed Sylvy to fight when there was a dead
kid metres away and a truce on the table? Why did nothing
feel enough? Why was nothing ever too much if it meant
she was with her Kings? Why was Saint always right?

All the abstracts came crashing down on the particulars and all was large and big and totally insurmountable, a string with no end working its way through her – Harry breathed and breathed and breathed and felt her lungs contract and her heartbeats like the footsteps of a giant on her eardrums and her blood congeal to beeswax and sting the skin from the inside. She clutched and grabbed at herself, trying to unburden, to unleash, to reveal, seeing the women in the posters doing similar, reaching down, reaching for, reaching under. She breathed. And breathed. And read the advertisements in an attempt at distraction: *Used Ford for sale, price negotiable... Upright piano. Will take offers.* Gradually, the crescendo waned, the staccato crimps of thought and blood-blushed cheeks ebbed. She breathed.

The clock told her ten minutes had blinked past. She checked herself: surprisingly intact, alive. A shadow lit the ground and the Crone shunted into the telephone booth.

'Alright in here?' she asked.

'Could you—' Harry began, feeling the rasp in her voice after its temporary dormancy in her throat. Behind the Crone, at the other end of a short corridor in the bar, Saint and Jackie were engaged in a debate with raised voices. Waiting, Harry assumed, for her to return. 'Could you tell them that... I need some time to clear my head.' The Crone nodded and turned with the message between her teeth. Harry grabbed her sleeve and stuttered, 'No, tell them that I'm missing the solitary confinement from prison, and I need some time alone because...'

'I'll just tell them you decided to leave.'

Harry patted the Crone on the upper arm and nodded.

'I'll see you later. When I'm more... myself.'

'Less yourself, you mean,' the Crone replied with a shimmer in her eye. After a final nod, Harry opened the back door and plunged into the night.

Ouisa showed no surprise when another girl came begging that night – but she was taken aback when this second girl accepted her ultimatum before she even reached the end of her sentence. *Where is it?* Harry had demanded, holding out her hand for the package that she had to deliver to Tottenham Court Road. What did she have to get where and *by when?*

Harry rehearsed Ouisa's instructions in her head as she strayed southwards, clenching the chunky envelope: *The club is called the Minted Tiger, on Tottenham Court Road. It's a gentleman's club. You've got two options for getting in – looking like a man or looking like a tart, it's up to you. In the back of the kitchen, there will be a staircase down to the club. Take it, and there's a door on your left, looks like a cupboard but it's an office, trust me. In there, you'll find an Irish kid*

*everyone calls Linchpin. Don't ask me why. Tell him that
Ouisa sent you, give it to him, and Bob's your uncle. When
he sends word that it's there, I'll be at your fight tomorrow.
The Kings, they'll be the next big thing, kid.*

Steering clear of Sisters' territory, and Kings' territory
too, she spilled out onto the long, dwindling Holloway
Road, stale neon in the early hours of the morning, veering
through empty market streets, round the industrial smash
of King's Cross. She walked the soles off her feet – like
that time, she thought, when she'd bitten her nails and
the flesh around them so much that she chewed herself
out of fingerprints; the police had settled for half-rounded
splotches smushed on the paper.

She stopped across the road from the Minted Tiger. A
throng of gentlemen semi-circled the black doors, next to
which a sign read *'MEN ONLY'* – just like, she thought,
the sign that read *'KINGS ONLY'* in one corner of The
Kings Head. A low-slung cloud near the entrance was
formed by the exhaled smoke of many men. Women were
entering through a side door; those women who beat the
pavements looking for crossings and touchings. The laws
changed so often now, these women were hazy themselves
on whether these half-dressed, better-kissed nights that
left their pockets full were criminal or merely frowned
upon. The doorman ushered them in and ushered them
out in equal measure.

198

Tart or man, that's how she could fit into this exclusive corner. Harry neared a bus stop and used the reflection of the glass to smear on layers of red lipstick. Still in her full white skirt and black, skin-tight top from the dance, she ripped it, lowering the neckline to show the tops of her non-existent breasts, gathering her waist into the tightest loop of her belt, showing off her stockinged legs. When she left the bus stop, altogether altered, a pile of shorn fabric and strands of hair were puddled on the ground, like someone had melted there.

Approaching the club once again, Harry saw another half-dressed, altogether-smudged lady exiting the venue from the red-awninged service door. Harry – although she didn't much feel like Harry anymore – rushed to catch it before the door shut. She shimmied through the gap. The leaving girl turned, wondering why there was no slam, and strung eyes with her replacement. Shrugging, she click-clacked away, letting the figure get to work.

A kitchen. Several waiters sprawled over shiny chrome worktops smoking butts. They leaned against plastic boxes of salad leaves and loopy-orange bread buns, whistling as the latest addition to the club walked past. Harry found the flight of stairs leading down into the belly of the club and scaled them with an oozing pleasure, shedding herself as she traced the red wallpaper with translucent fingers. The plush of heavy, unusual music, of strings and brass, upheld itself louder and louder as she progressed downwards.

She surveyed the nightmare around her. Men chatting with men laughing with men, watching women dance with women to the tune of a rocky velvet song and a vodka on the rocks and two clocks saying the hour was early in the morning, the wives were fast asleep and would barely notice the door-clunk as they arrived home. Men laughing loudly, their guffaws drowning out any semblance of wit or distaste for each other. Unlike the regal burgundy of The Kings Head, this room was a shadowy red, the bloodied mouth of a wildcat, unbearable. Hired girls took to the stage in turns, wearing clothes that went out of fashion years ago, flapper dresses, corsets, petticoats, bushy skirts. The men dressed like speakeasy-goers, as though time herself had wound backwards and dumped them here for their Saturday night entertainment. Waiters performed elaborate figures of eight, gliding between tables like needles pulling thread, sewing the club together with lust and money and drink. No friendly bartenders. Tart, man, whatever – the only thing for women to be here was an object.

But Harry had a job to do: suddenly single-minded again, everything else falling out of her line of worry, she scanned the space. The young red-headed man stood in the nearest doorway caught her eye: his arms crossed, eyes flitting around the room. Very young – someone's child, she thought. Harry slithered towards him, sticking to the shadows and the spaces behind columns.

'Did I order you?' he asked, his gaze smearing her body as she planted it in front of him.

'Are you Linchpin?' she replied.

'Who's asking?'

'Ouisa sent me.'

He jerked his head to the office and she followed him inside. Handed over the package. Harry had left her head somewhere in Camden – it was certainly nowhere to be found in that back office – and the next day, when she tried to remember it, she couldn't even tell herself what colour the walls were and whether there had been one, two or three men sniffing powder at the back of the room. She must have left the package though, and it must have been alright, because before long she'd been spat out into the club again. She was certain she was about to leave, her foot had been on the stairs – when a hand pulled her back in.

A man with greasy teeth and a stomach large enough for him to rest his hands on offered to buy her a drink. Did he know her, Harry wondered, followed by the worst kind of reassurance: no one knew her here. She was no one here. And because Harry would have said *no*, she said *yes*. She had said *yes* to Ouisa because Mr George would have wanted her to say *no*. Because her mother had wanted her to be responsible, she had done the opposite. Woman. Man. Father. Son. Cousin. Tart. Girlfriend. Sister. Brother. All these shitty particulars had cored her out. How was she supposed to recognize herself when everyone was telling her what she looked like? She had been too busy trying to fit into one or another of those words that the Kings were her haven where she became Harry – and now that was buckling under disaster, was dying out, who would she be after it ended? In a world where she was nothing, the Kings made her something. Without their streets, without the Kings, she would be nothing once more.

He led her to a table in the corner where no one could see them and asked for her price. She laughed and he liked that – he liked it a lot. *People say the funny ones are no fun, but I disagree*, he whispered to her, as if sharing a secret. The music roiled around them and Edie came into her mind; the way she used to say *hey, you* in anger, then *come here* with a smile, and how Harry had scrambled to follow her, Tony by her side, when she was Petie and Nell's age; and how the raindrops had clung to Edie's lips as she told her about *him*, the man that made her want to take Finsbury Park by the scruff of its neck. *I should have seen him coming*, she'd said. *He told me that the funny ones are what he liked.*

Whisky after whisky put on the table in front of her and she drank them all unblinking. The man asked if she wanted to dance, and she refused. He leaned forwards and the wash of his cigar-breath reminded Harry of her father as she last saw him, curled at the head of a wire bedframe, his chest craning under coughs, his yellow teeth; that face like hers, round as the moon's, and the paleness of his cheeks when the blood could no longer make it there to refill them, blood in his shredded-coconutty moustache, peppered with grey and black and brown. She demanded another drink, and her partner obliged.

The furniture took on blurs, and chandeliers threw their rays down too fast; she sloshed further into what she was realizing was danger. An announcer came to the stage and said the final show was beginning. *Here, sit next to me, right here*, the man said and nestled her in beside him. Girls engaged in fake fights on stage, which got the crowd jeering, moaning, having too much fun restraining themselves. The performers gradually took off layers, beginning in overcoats and hats, ending in lingerie. Harry wondered if their very innards might soon be on display. The man started snaking his arm around her shoulders.

Terror lunged in her and she pushed the man's arm back so hard he smacked himself in the face. He shouted for help. She was *out of control, running wild*. Running from his voice, Harry flew towards the stairs, the kitchen, retracing her steps out of the club. She leaned all her weight on the side door, gasping the clean night air, as she continued running, running. Her mind was laps ahead and she didn't know how to catch up to it with her legs alone. She raced after the tail end of it, chasing down dawn.

Tony, 2017

'Did you know?' I point to the sheet of paper – 'CLOSING SUNDAY' – sellotaped to the door.

Saint shakes her head, wincing as she puts a hand to her neck and starts rubbing. She's told me before that her neck has never been the same since 1957. Her husband thinks that's just a saying; I know it's the truth. I watched someone stamp on it and crunch her glasses into the mud for good measure.

'Why would I know?' she asks. Unsaid: we have no official connection to this place. No one would email us, or notify us, or call us to let us know, not even out of kindness.

'There's nothing we can do to stop it, anyway. I spoke to the kid at the bar. The sale is finalized, deal done. We're late to the party.'

Saint asks me something, but the sound of celebrations as Man United scores a goal drowns her out. When the men quieten down, she asks again.

'Why would we want to stop it?'

'I thought you'd want… you know…'

'No, I don't.'

Fear of stilted conversation drifts out; there's no room between us for that. Saint demands the answer of me. Meeting for one day a year means 'get it off your chest'. And one day is all we can afford. It's enough to keep the time alive, keep the ball in play for another few paces. But too much time together and we would sink back into the guilt, no longer be able to deny that we weren't like *that*, we weren't capable of *that*; certainty is so much easier to impose from a distance.

'Well, because it means something to us.' I gesture around, not sure at what: the jackpot machines, the television screens, the stale-piss smell. She follows my hand, wondering what I'm gesturing at too.

'Something, yes. But not everything.'

'I don't understand, Saint.' Then, after a pause: 'You were the one who started these reunions, weren't you?'

I figure the time for denial is long past. We'll deny it out of existence if we're not careful. I had long suspected that Saint penned the article, not only from its well-written, polite enquiry framed in dinner-table *could-you-maybe*s, but also the hungry look in her eyes when I sat across the table from her for the first time in years; desperate to return to the past. We all took our leave of the Kings, in some way or another, but Saint sooner than most. At a dance hall somewhere north of here, she fell into the arms of a man who had fought overseas. She fell for the argyle socks peeking out from under his Royal Air Force-assigned trousers, the precision of his crew cut. She fell for him, and she fell for the idea of qualifying as a lawyer. She fell pregnant though – and when she went back to the practice where she had started as a junior associate, her colleagues were associates, and when they made partner she was still junior associate, and when they started their own firms she watched them shaking hands from the other side of the glass-walled office, cutting their cake for them and handing out slices. She told me that a single moment came into her mind as she carried over the paper plates, bent under the weight of the sponge: Harry tearing through the arcade, smashing the nearest windows and leaving behind her a trail of glittering glass.

'You wanted to bring us back here,' I say.

'Back together, full-stop. The pub was just a convenient place to meet. The hall is gone, and that didn't change anything did it?'

'The hall's not *gone*.'

'It might as well be,' she says.

She's right: Harfleur Hall – the place where we swapped partners in excuse-me dances, creeped our way from nine to midnight, where Elvis reigned supreme, and our majesty unmatched – is gone. After it was a dance hall, it became a concert hall, then years ago, without any fanfare, they turned it into a church: modern, clinical, turquoise, advertising its brand of faith on the side. If only those congregations knew, as they sat pious and pitiful, that we'd used that floor to bless ourselves as youths, that others had used it later to worship the guitar twangs of Hendrix and Bowie and screamed until their lungs were empty and their livers full.

Saint's eyes meet mine, both of us wondering if there's still that shiny patch on the floorboards, blood rotting somewhere in the deeper grooves from where someone was cut between grooves. Rites of communion above an indelible stain.

I feel myself working to follow Saint's line of thought – she always was the smartest of us all. When we had shrugged around phrases like *she's sort of not one of us*, we had never meant it, but I notice her quick cover-ups and swerves in conversations; an instinct bedded deep inside her, scars to the bone.

'You're the only one who calls me Saint, still,' she smiles, knowing that's why I do it. Someone has to.

The men erupt again at the table behind us, still not leaving the woman alone to drink her water. Saint swivels in her chair to look.

'I already tried,' I say. 'She doesn't want our help.'

'I wouldn't want my help either,' Saint says in return. She smiles, crinkles bunching up around her eyes, behind the bright blue, acrylic glasses. I believe that she could still land a punch, if she wanted to.

'Maybe she doesn't know she needs it.'

'Maybe she *doesn't* need it.'

'Remember when...' I start.

'Yes... when I first came in here. Huffing, puffing—'

'Crying—'

'Alright, don't milk it!'

'And Harry told you that joke.' Her face drops at the mention of Harry, but I pick it back up for her. It feels good to be passengers on the same train of thought: the woman with her water, an offer of help, Saint's first time in this pub, running from heckles that came from behind.

'What do you call a blue that's not as heavy as all the other blues?'

The punchline is too instant and we egg each other on to cave and say it. It comes out at a similar time; we whisper it, almost as though Harry will hear us if we're not careful. Saint is still afraid of her, I think.

'Light blue.'

'It used to make Jackie laugh too.' Saint grins.

'Is she coming?'

Saint looks up.

'You didn't hear?' Saint pauses, leaving me to fill in the blanks. 'All that smoking finally caught up with her.'

'It seems she caught up with Leslie after all, as well. Those two always were chasing after one another.'

'And chasing after Harry...' Saint trailed off, shaking her head. She touches her neck more tenderly, with an achy smile on her face.

'We *all* followed after Harry.'

'Yes, but...' Saint blinks at me. 'Oh, come on, Tony. Jackie was besotted with Harry. You really didn't notice?'

'No,' I reply, in total truth. Harry had all but hypnotized me, secluded us in a world where nothing else mattered but her word and her direction. She dangled wars and rivalries, tit-for-tats, so close to my face that I couldn't see past them.

'I remember when she—' Saint starts laughing before she reaches the memory. I reach over and touch it for her.

'Yes, when Jackie punched a kid because he called Harry a boy—'

'Which wasn't an insult—'

'Not to Harry—'

'But she did it anyway, and Harry thanked her for it—'

'Just to make her feel better.'

Our laugh and talk blend into each other. The memories grow legs and walk around us, all over the crappy carpets.

The men are still causing the woman problems, and she's shifting in her seat, glancing out the window. One of them has started to fondle her forearm and ask her who she's waiting for and whether it's him.

'I'm going to have to say something. There's no shame in accepting some help once in a while.' I see this all the time, tightly wound girls taught independence to the extent that accepting an offer of help is a crime. You have to smack them over the head with your friendly hand, extort them into accepting companionship. It's like sisterhood has become a trick.

'Tony, don't, she doesn't want it.' Saint shakes her head.

'I can't let her sit there and squirm.'

I stand up from my chair and groan it backwards. Saint clutches at my wrist. The door blows open and another young woman strides in. The woman at the table's eyes soar up, thankful: evidently, they're friends. Pausing in the doorway, she scans the pub, making quick calculations about the men at the table.

'Want to try this other place down the road?' she asks casually, hand still on the door. Her friend jumps up and saunters out without looking back, the men turning mute back to their football match. I lower myself into the chair. Saint and I sit there in shock, some embarrassment. There was never going to be a fight.

FOURTEEN

'Stand still or I'll stab you!' Morgan yelled, fastening a brooch onto Bonbon's lapel. Her chubby, red-freckled fingers fumbled with the jewellery and she gave Bonbon a light prick in the heart. Bonbon *ow*-ed, and Morgan flicked the air playfully in response before turning and examining herself, standing so close to the full-length mirror that this sleek-suited woman obscured the background.

The Seven Sisters had claimed the front room of Tomson's Tailors. It was common knowledge that Tomson went to his brother's home in Walthamstow for Sunday lunch, leaving his tailors and the flat above empty. The Sisters knew the teenager who had just started working in the back, sewing for her keep. The Cypriot kid – dark-haired, cinnamon-skinned, eyes wide to take in the new – lived in Kings' territory. With some rough words, Morgan had crept under the Bridge and persuaded the little seamstress to open Tomson's door with her emergency key and give them access to the front room, and its racks of clothing.

Tomson's was cluttered with pots of needles, sewing machines, glue guns, all manner of tools. When she entered for the first time, Morgan imagined the cumulative pain of a thousand needles, the drumming of the sewing machine pulsating into the soft, fatty babyflesh still clinging to her underchin, and shuddered. The moment passed as she turned her attention to the spools of coloured thread that wound themselves tightly on colour-organized shelves. Jars of buttons, delectably arranged, looked edible. Rails of suits, crisp, ironed, altered, fashionable and fashioned, waited for collection tomorrow morning. The surrounding street was empty. On the corner of Fonthill and Lennox, Tomson's Tailors was invisible.

'Did you hear about Ouisa?' The bell-ringing door swung closed behind Joey. Morgan shook hands with her; Joey patted Laurie on the shoulder; Bonbon shouldered Morgan. The Seven Sisters, bumping into one another, connecting and interconnecting, joining, unjoining and rejoining, were readying; last night – nearly – forgotten.

'I heard Ouisa was back with the Kings.'

'I'll believe that when I see it.'

'I bet you ten shillings that Ouisa shows up for the Sisters,' Morgan said, offering her hand. Joey smiled and shook it. Laurie sighed loudly from across the room, seated in Tomson's chair.

213

'I'm sticking to fists, I've decided.' She stood up. 'A good, honest fight.' As the newest of the Sisters, still imprinting her impression, she had been working up to this announcement for weeks.

'That's how it goes anyway.' Morgan raised her knuckles at Laurie. 'Everybody decides that this is the first line of defence. But the first line gets quickly replaced by the second.' She took out a knuckle duster and slotted it onto her fingers. 'And the second becomes the third.' She took a switchblade out of her pocket. 'I can tell you've not done one of these before, Laurie.' She turned away and admired the new brooch on Bonbon's lapel. The smoky black faux jewel was surrounded by seven spiky petals in rusty brass-gold, the shape of a sinful sun, or a deadly flower.

'If we win today—'

'When.' Joey turned from where she riffled through the suits on the rack for collection, measuring the sleeve lengths against her own.

'If we win, then we should get matching brooches made.'

'Why?'

'Because, you know… for the Seven Sisters. Not just the girlfriends anymore, but the real deal.'

Silence swept through the tailors, before Joey broke it.

'Matching jewellery?' she grimaced.

The door banged open, the bell *ding-a-ling*ed. Sylvy and Char entered, bickering.

Also bickering, Petie and Nell stood in the alley behind The Kings Head.

'But what did she *look* like!'

'I didn't see her face, she was wearing a hat,' Petie returned to Nell.

Neither of them had slept. Neither had tried. A weak sun cooled the day – but the two were shivering long before they ventured out into the cold. Petie had remained out in it all night, flitting between the Dent and random doorways on the Terrace, too terrified to go home to the small flat where her mother would spy the blood on her shirt. She had watched the inevitable gasp and scolding and suspicion over and over in her mind and decided she didn't need to see it come true. A street-walking woman, a prostitute perhaps, had disturbed Petie. She shot up to tell her to *bugger off* because her kind weren't welcome here. From the shadows, the woman asked Petie about her blood-soaked sleeve and her streaming nose and red-raw eyes. Petie explained she'd had a bad night, and that she had to do something tomorrow that she might never be able to undo, that was all.

Nell was having a hard time believing her – about the woman, about what she said, about anything.

'How do you even know it was a *prostitute*? You said you didn't see them.'

'It doesn't matter, but they *told* me not to look back.' Petie crossed her arms.

'Is that before or after they told you where to find the yellow-brick road?' Nell said, also with her arms crossed.

The two turned their backs on each other and paced the small yard where white sheets on washing lines fluttered in to separate them.

'You don't believe me,' Petie murmured. Nell was too far away to hear. 'But she *told* me to join them today. We have to. *I* have to.' She paused, the alley silent. 'Nell, where are you?'

'Where's Harry?' Tony asked Leslie as she tumbled through the door of The Kings Head, face ashen with worry. 'Did you lose her?'

'Oh, that's rich. I *found* her this morning, didn't I? And I told her what you discussed last night – that there's extra coppers on the streets today, that anywhere around Harfleur is strictly off limits. She's…'

'She's what?'

'She went after Ouisa last night.'

'We were supposed to *wait*,' Jackie plunged in.

'I suppose Harry couldn't…' Leslie trailed off and moved over to the bar. The Kings Head was bereft, colourless – woolly grey outside the windows, woollen greys and blacks on their bodies. The pub only opened for five hours on a Sunday, a few hours at lunch and a few hours in the evening. They had hit the gap, when the pub was theirs, barricading them against the world outside.

'Look at the state of you,' Tony sighed, nearly pulling the lapels off Leslie's jacket.

'Leave it out.' Leslie pushed off her hands. 'It'll be messed up in a few hours anyway.'

'Where's Harry?' Saint asked, entering, pencil in hand, as if ready to write on the walls.

'I don't know, but she went fishing for Ouisa last night.'

Saint's jaw dropped. 'That's *my* plan. *Ahead* of schedule. I spent weeks buttering Ouisa up for the right moment.'

'Well, Harry obviously thinks that's now.'

'That's the last time I make plans for Harry to throw them out the bloody window.' She waved her finger in Tony's face, before lowering it. The two girls shared a glance, knowing. Saint began counting to ten in little mumbles.

'Why didn't I hem these trousers?' Jackie said, looking at where her trousers reached the ground.

'Because you think you're taller than you are,' Leslie joked.

'Just get me some scissors from that drawer. I'm going to snip them for now and sew them up tidier when the rumble's over tonight.' Leslie leaned over the bar, grabbing the implement to make the cut.

'They're gathering already,' Sylvy announced, jumping straight into business.

'Have you seen Ouisa?' Morgan asked. 'Is she with them?'

'She won't be fighting with us today.' Char, sullen, looked at the floor. Sylvy squeezed her elbow gently, as if acknowledging a secret held in her body.

'Where's my ten shillings?' Joey held out her hand.

'Hold your horses.' Morgan pointed a finger. 'I haven't seen it yet.'

'We've got something else to say.' Char stood with her back to the Sisters, scanning the deserted streets outside the window.

'We?' Morgan asked. Char and Sylvy shared a look and left the pronoun dangling in the air.

'Sylvy is taking over.'

'I wouldn't say *taking over*. It's just that now I don't have to listen to what Char says anymore, not if I don't want to.'

'But my final request was that...'

'We'll try and stop the fight.' Sylvy gritted her teeth. The two girls began unspooling the plan, interchanging responses and announcements in organized stitches of talk that threaded together into something resembling leadership.

'We're going to talk,' Char explained. 'Nobody wants a fight, not after what happened last night. It's not us. We're better than the boys. Or at least, we should try and be better than those idiots.'

'We don't want another dead kid in Islington. Not because of us. There's more to think about than rivalry.'

'Is there?' Bonbon fizzled. She was playing with Tomson's drawer of scissors, running her hand along the silver blades.

'Yes!' Petie shouted. 'We have to be there.'

Nell slapped her hand on the brick. The two had found each other in the murky afternoon after several sulked minutes. If Petie wasn't here, then Nell would have been at home by now. All she wanted was to lock her door, crawl under her covers, and forget what Harry's face looked like – its curves and freckles and scars. But Petie was here, just as much as Bernadette wasn't. In the wad of air between their glances, she wasn't here; in the quiet between their sentences, she wasn't here; in the stillness between their arms, she wasn't here. Nell wished that Saint had never come to her at the school gates, and she wished she had never gone to Petie with the offer. She should have kept her mouth shut. She had to unravel the mistake she'd knotted them in, and save Petie. She had seen Tony do more for Harry.

'What about Bernie?' she mumbled.

'We couldn't have done anything about that.' Petie did the turn and sniff that meant she was betraying tears just below the surface. 'You heard what Harry said last night, eye for an eye, making them pay and all that.' Petie gripped her hands. Passion gleamed in her eyes. 'We can get them back for what they did. We can show that we're Kings.'

'Which will mean *what*?'

'It means…' Petie whispered. 'That we'll be the same as anyone else on these streets. We'll be untouchable.'

Nell paused. Petie held onto her hands.

'Alright… I'm doing this for Bernie though.' And for Petie. And the tiniest part of her, for herself. Being untouchable, she had to admit, sounded good.

'It sounds good.' Tony patted on the bar.

Saint continued: 'The Sisters will try to stop us from fighting, offer us some half-baked deal, because they'll want an early night and a quick way out. We've got to make Harry take the deal. With Ouisa on our side, we need to be acting smart. Harry has upped the stakes. She's made it a fight for the spotlight.' Saint gestured to the smoggy grey outside the window where the first few smacks of rain were hitting the ground. 'Even the day doesn't want us to fight. It's started to spit at us....'

'Saint could be right.' Tony nodded.

'God, are you sober, Tony?' Saint smiled.

'So, how do we get Harry to shake someone's hand instead of cutting it off?'

'How do we get Harry to *talk*?'

'Harry loves to talk,' Char laughed. 'It's all she does. You just need to get her going.'

'What about all the Sisters...' Morgan began, 'who *wanted* to fight. Who've rolled out for the afternoon, dressed for victory, and thinking of the bottled anger they can tip all over the Patch... come on, Sylvy... could you take that away from them?' The vision glittered in her eyes. She pretended – though the room knew the truth – that she was talking about Sisters other than herself.

'I agree with Morgan,' Bonbon said.

'They'll have to forget about that—'

'The only thing you need to agree with is *us*.'

'We don't know what the numbers will be,' Sal moaned from the corner. 'How many others will have decided to turn King, like Ouisa?'

'They say it's going to be nearly five to one,' Petie tattled as she entered the pub. Nell skulked in behind her, catching the swinging door before it hit her in the face.

The Kings tried to protest.

'It's true. We heard someone telling someone else that Sylvy was boasting about the numbers.'

'*That* someone probably told someone else times two,' Saint cut in. 'Besides, how does she know who's going to show up? Where did she buy her crystal ball?'

'Didn't Harry nick a crystal ball for Edie once?'

'No, that was a good luck charm.'

'With a bit of luck, this shouldn't be too hard,' Joey concluded. She was throwing around a spool of cotton with Bonbon, trying not to unravel it in the process. 'The Kings mostly just sit around their own campfire, telling themselves stories.'

'Remember that time we went to the Cutty Sark and swung on the sails?' Morgan tried an impression of Tony, pouting her lips in the way that the Marilyn-wannabe did and twisting strands of hair around her ginger-freckled finger. The impression fell flat.

'Remember that time we rumbled so hard that the ground shook under our very feet?' Bonbon tried an impression of Harry, stuffing out her chest and talking in that loud, wavering voice that hitched on someone's soul.

'Remember that time we cut that bad movie short in the Astoria by stealing the projector?' Joey had a final go at Harry, twisting herself full of hate, but they all knew that no impression could come close.

'Remember that time Harry stole a car, drove it around for two days, gave us all lifts, put it back where it was, and nobody even noticed?' Jackie mused.

'It's still there, I think,' Tony said. 'Parked on the corner where it always is. Either nobody owns it, or they just don't drive it.'

'Who drives in this neck of the woods anyway?' Jackie asked.

'Harry,' everybody replied.

Sal had snagged a sewing kit from Tomson's desk and was licking and re-licking the end of the thread, trying to get it through the eye of the needle. She busied her hands to block out the name Ouisa going back and forth across the room. At that name, she heard only deep regret surge within her. If only she had known turning King was an option. She should have gone to the Kings, Sal realized, while deep in the Seven Sisters territory and far too late. She should have – like Ouisa – pinballed across the streets to another gang. Harry would have protected her from what was coming.

The topic of switching sides came up on the night she spilled to Harry about Bert. The leader of the Kings had come to see her and apologize for the night in the pub. *I didn't mean to scare you, Sal, you know me...* she muttered in the windowless corridor outside Sal's flat. *It's just these girls... I care so much about them, I'd kill for them.* Harry had scared herself with that statement. *You know how I am, I get carried away sometimes.* And she had carried Sal with her, all the way to the nearest milk bar and the bottoms of their glasses, ten memories deep. Without prompting, Sal had started talking about Bert's involvement with the Sisters; Harry asked her questions about it, egged her on, and afterwards, she thanked her – *her*, no-one Sal, pinball Sal, short-arse Sal. She should have joined the Kings then and there. Who knew why she hadn't. Perhaps it had something to do with Harry's smile, like a panther ready to pounce.

Sal was still in her Sunday suit. She had accompanied her mother to the church, taking turns to hold her baby brother on her lap and bounce him up and down, up and down, until the ball of her foot got sore on the cold stone floor.

She continued twiddling the needle, but there was no jacket on her lap, nothing in need of stitching. Briefly, she imagined herself sewing the grey, buffering air to the street corner, hoping the needle would be strong enough to pierce the tarmac and still time in stitches.

Saint regarded the muffled grey outside the window, a dusky Victorian fog that refused to lift with the times. She sat at the bar, making an elaborate battle diagram, like a coach before a big match, plotting game plans. The page was so full of cross-cutting scribbles and joined-up lines that it combed itself into a wash of single scratchings. Little circles marked with letters and numbers overlapped and duplicated themselves until the paper was an alphabetized blizzard of single, white obscurity.

'Why do I bother?' Saint crumpled up the paper in her hand. Tony, appearing from behind, patted her on the shoulder.

'If you didn't bother, no one would.' Tony paused, then continued. 'Jackie told me about last night… you and Harry.'

'I don't want to talk about it. We were both high on… the rush, or something.'

'I don't blame you. It's about time our very own Saint Joan finally snapped, after all these years of Harry's endless… endless…'

'There's not quite a word for it, is there?' Saint crunched her brow.

'Not for Harry, no.'

'Thanks,' Saint said. Tony gave her shoulder two more pats, before turning to Petie and Nell and shouting:

'Oi, you two!'

'What?' Char and Sylvy looked up from their head-knocking closeness.

'We should be going, shouldn't we?' Morgan pointed to the clock. 'Why are we hanging about in this needle-den?'

'Harry's going to meet us there,' Tony said, ushering them out. 'I'm not waiting around for her anymore.'

Jackie and Leslie were already on the doorstop, lighting cigarettes, talking in hushed voices.

'...why would one feel like that and one not? It doesn't—' Leslie caught herself at the sight of Tony. She silenced her sister with a shushing stare.

The evening behind them was tipping, nearly with rain, mainly with time well gone. With a click, the day had passed. Night was here. The Kings moved towards the battleground, slapping each other on the back, yelping bravado that dissolved on air.

'Couldn't cool us down if you *tried*.'

'We're hot enough to burn the Kings to the ground.' Morgan smacked the closest wall.

'Where is Harry, anyhow? She's better at all this.'

'All what?'

'All the conversations we have to go through.' Sal shook her head. 'How we like to offend the Kings from top to bottom, from head to toe… their clothes, their shoes, their hair. Then we move on to their mothers, their fathers, their little brothers, their ways of saying hello, their ways of saying goodbye.'

'How will we fit all those things in?' Joey said in sarcasm. 'We'd better start.'

A distant giggle hightailed over the roofs. 'Don't be so cocky. You'll look chicken,' they said.

'Shall we give them a head start?'

'There she is. There's Harry,' they said.

'Look, there's Ouisa with her!'

'What a suit. Shame to ruin it,' they said.

'Her *hair*.'

Harry was sweating – but no one could tell. Even as the Kings grew nearer to the Dent and began kicking up the dust, clapping Harry on the back, complimenting her hair, offering cigarettes, offering lights and stars and all the moons in between, none of them could sense the clammy underarmness Harry shifted in her shirt to avoid. She nodded, smiled, accepted the cigarettes, while a trickle of backsweat glid down her spine; took secret moments to wipe her hands on her trouser legs and pull in her arms to mop up the puddles growing in her armpits.

Fifteen or so had turned out: including Ouisa, who lingered off to the side with Roz, talking in sign. The Kings, in their black Sunday suits, milling about like peppercorns on the bomb-cut floor, surveyed her quickly in turn; no one wanted to be seen looking at her, relying on her, hoping on her.

Saint didn't try to hide that she was expecting more. She grabbed the rolled cigarette paper and began totting up and tallying the Kings present, chewing on the end of an already stubbed pencil, her lips and teeth turning the colour of lead as the day progressed. She tutted nervously. Sweat was visible on her upper lip.

'We could have done with a couple more, don't you think?' Leslie asked under her breath. 'I know we've got Ouisa, but what's *one* when you're still outnumbered. Where are they all now?'

'Don't talk like that, Les,' Harry upped her volume; the Kings turned their heads towards her, focused. 'It's clear we're the only ones who care enough about these streets.' Harry shared a glance with Ouisa. 'If ten or fifteen or whatever is all we can get, then it's what we'll take, and take it happily. The more drinks to go around afterwards.' She caught eyes with a fidgeting Nell. Nell looked down. 'And if anyone is chicken... sorry, not willing to fight, if anyone wants to go home, you're more than welcome to go. I won't hold it against you. I've got cab fares for every-one, right here in my pocket.' Harry yanked her jacket, making the coins in her pocket clink loudly.

The offer dwindled in the air like a lazy balloon. No one dared move.

'I promise, cross my heart. I'd close my eyes, so I didn't know who went. You could still be a King. This turf would be yours as much as mine.'

'Harry... nobody wants to go,' Saint nudged her after a quiet moment. Harry set her lips and nodded.

'Alright then, what day is it today?'

'It's Sunday,' Jackie supplied.

'Right. That's right. And every Sunday from today, whether you're in church or at home or wherever, you'll think of this Sunday. When you see that mark on your face... I've already got two,' Harry walked through the crowd, pointing at a paper-white, thumbnail-sized curve just below her lip, and another smaller, browner crease on her rounded jaw, '... when you look at them in a mirror, or in a photo, or in the reflection of a bus, you can be honest with yourself or whoever's asking, and you can share the story of what happened today. Miles in the future, if someone asks where the scars are from, you can lie, if you want to. You can say it's from when you were a kid in the bomb ruins and you tripped over all the time and cut open your leg. I won't come for you in your memories. But if you're a true King, you'll remember where it's from. You'll know. In donkeys, when we're old and split to the other ends of the country, we'll remember, *won't* we? If you walk past the Patch or this Dent, you'll hear my words... you *will*, I guarantee you.' She shunted out the words, as if the Kings would have to obey them just from their force. Desperation winked in her eye; a fury not quite burned off. 'Others will forget, others won't know what happened today, but that won't matter as long as *we* do. We won't, us few girls.'

'Too right,' Petie chorused.

Harry's wash of unkempt speaking – the longest speech the Kings had heard from her – ended with shouts of support and vigorous nods from the informal audience. In their heads, the gang burned the speech into memory, razing patches on the dark side of their skull where those words could remain forever.

'It's nearly six,' Saint whispered through the foray into Harry's ear. 'It's time.' Harry pushed Saint and her time away. A policeman walked past the Dent. The Kings hushed at his bobbing face. He checked his watch and kept walking. Harry looked up at the bruise-coloured sky.

'I've got an idea.' Harry smiled. 'Get the camera!'

'Why do you want that? It's nearly dark.'

'Go on, get it!' Tony hissed to Jackie.

'What for?'

'To snap this.' Harry tried to point everywhere all at once, as if to pin down the air.

Jackie set off running down the street. For two short years in the war, their mother had worked for a unit in northern Africa, documenting the day-to-day and sharing films of British victories on the western front to unenthusiastic audiences. She received a Rolleicord camera for her troubles, and this had become Jackie's, and then the Kings', camera. Jackie rarely developed the photos, but on that film rested the negative evidence of their lives. She returned a moment later from her flat, which was within eyeshot of the Dent, with a leather bag strung about her shoulder. The strange black box, with its two goggling lenses, drew eyes; the youngsters had never seen one.

Harry grabbed it from Jackie and told the Kings to climb onto the burnt and brittle rafters of the Dent's carcass. They followed the directions. Tony and Saint crossed arms and stood at one end. Jackie and Leslie clambered into open gaps, sitting and grinning, swinging their legs over the side. Petie and Nell, with Harry's insistence, shuffled their way up, along the beams and into frame. The rafters creaked.

'Nobody else can get on, it'll crumble!' Saint yelled, grabbing a beam. The rest remained in the rubble. Those in Harry's viewfinder set their faces good as stone, while she climbed onto a jaggedy wall on the other side of the street to gain vantage and a semi-omniscient point of view. She looked into the portal, adjusted the lens, and snapped. From this moment onwards, nothing was clear.

FIFTEEN

Despite pleading from both sides, the final gambit failed. The fight was on.

The girls filed onto Andover Patch, as arranged. It was little more than a square of arid grass roughly half the size of a football pitch, which leaked into Seven Sisters territory, and had once belonged to the Kings. Four newly built and triangle-shaped blocks of flats fenced the Patch into an arena, a council-funded colosseum. Half-hearted landscaping meant scruffy hedgerows and angled benches had once neatly quartered the grass, but the residents had since moved those perfect borders into a mishmash of obstacles. It was nearly full dark: even if people decided to watch from nearby balconies, they would see only a mesh of tangled fabrics moving and faltering on the grass. The Kings and the Sisters kept to opposite diagonal corners, murmuring to themselves like smacks of jellyfish, neither assertive enough to make the first move.

From where Tony stood beside Harry, surveying the Patch, she saw an unplayed chess board, the moveless space. Countless matches at the back of The Kings Head had always left her with the feeling that, however practised and prepared she was, she could not control her opponent's moves. Or perhaps it was Mrs Patrick who had told her something along those lines at the back of the textiles classroom, when she shoved the book about Paris into Tony's hands and told her to *defy the odds*. Now, Tony tried to consider the odds, the moves, the openings, to figure out her opponent. It didn't seem to be the Sisters, but rather the night itself and the unravelled time lying before them. It made her wonder whether the game was worth playing at all.

She pulled on Harry's arm and took her aside, noticing the waxy sheen on her paler-than-usual face.

'You look bloody awful,' she whispered. 'Where have you been all night?'

'I had an errand to run.'

'You've not been home, have you?' Harry's hair was askew, her face shining with moisture from deep inside her pores, all the way from her liver; eyes grey and dreary, fizzling with energy that should have been burned up in dreams by now. 'The others can't tell, but I can, Harry. If you're not sure, if you want to call this off, then we can. It's not too late to go back. And we'll fight again. The Kings will keep on and we can prove ourselves another time.'

Harry looked hard ahead.

'If there is another time,' she said. Tony wondered what the night had done to her friend. 'Are you sober?' Harry asked. A nod. 'Got your prayers in?' Tony rolled her eyes. 'I'm surprised you're not like Leslie, wishing we had more.'

'You know as much as I do that if we could fight this just you and me, then we would.'

Harry nodded.

'I know.'

'And I don't even know why I'd do it,' Tony continued. She phrased it cautiously, trying to work her way through to an answer. 'So long as you were doing it, I'd be there.'

'I know,' Harry said, mournfully. Tony went quiet. Their impending and inevitable separation became very loud. Continuing, afraid of the enlightenment welling up in her, Tony said:

'You know everything, but please…' She kneaded her hand into the shoulder pad of Harry's suit. 'Please don't be an idiot. If you hear the coppers, *run*. Not like what happened in the summer, when you stood there on the doorstep waiting for them to pick you up.' Harry started to deny it, but Tony stared at her with a flat mouth until she stopped. 'It was hard enough for them without you for two months. If you went for any longer, the Kings would be dust – and there might be a time when I'm not there to stop you from being an idiot. Please, this time, *run*. For me.'

'Look at you, telling me what to do… are you going to hit me with a cricket bat again?'

Tony grabbed Harry's unfeeling hand; their faces were sombre, funereal. Something had been finished here. The chess match was already over, the pieces swept off the board.

'Everything alright over here, ladies?' Ouisa asked, picking at her nails. Pretending indifference. She spat a lob of something onto the grass. 'Perhaps it's not the time to be sharing our favourite recipes and saying how much we love each other. When's it all going to kick off?'

'Oi!' Sylvy's voice rang out from across the Patch. Ouisa gestured for Harry to go, and she slouched across the grass towards Sylvy, smiling back at Tony. Fog built around them.

'Rules?' Sylvy asked, meeting the rival leader in the centre.

'First side to scatter loses.'

'Weapons?'

'Anything… knives.'

'Bats?'

'Chains.'

'The lot,' Harry cut her off. Sylvy forced her head to bend, as if to royalty. It began as suddenly as someone rips open curtains to let in the light.

'Get off, get off!' Nell wriggled under a black-booted Sister who had a nasty snarl on her face. She pressed down, squishing Nell into the wettening mud, spattered with new rain. Petie clocked them and tackled the Sister to the floor with a *thunk*. Both girls lay there stunned for several seconds while sharp raindrops cut their faces – before Petie wrenched herself from the floor and shoved her scrappy shoe on the Sister's shoulder. Petie, thinking thoughts of *for Bernie, for Bernie* and *shoe's on the other foot now, eh?*, grinned down at the bug she had pinned to the ground.

Nell brushed herself off and stood beside her friend, looking down at the Sister. She picked mud from her mouth; her body was already battered with nudges and slams. This cluster was on the fringe of the brawl, nearly against one of the buildings.

'I think we should...'

'Don't say it.' Petie held a finger up at Nell, almost on her lips.

'We should let her go. I don't...' Nell dabbed at her bleeding, wobbling lip. 'I don't want to be here, Petie.' She checked behind her. Far out of the lens, Harry flailed. One took on three. Even at a good squint, she was just a swig of a person. To the balcony-clingers, the bird's-eye viewers, these were reckless street youth trashing the estate's reputation; to the papers, the wrack of the modern waves; to themselves, hard-working girls, war kids, fighting to defend something that felt good to have.

The Sister squirmed under Petie's shoe.

'I'll let her go for everything in her pockets.' Petie's voice was like frozen iron, stolen from warmth. She didn't take her eyes off Nell.

'Petie, that's… that's not fair.'

'Give me the lot.' Petie held out her hand to the girl under her foot, who whimpered, mumbling that she needed the money in her pockets. She couldn't do without it. Please, please, please. Petie kept her hand stuck out, pressed her foot down harder. Nell pleaded with her too. The whimpers dried out as the rain pelted them, growing heavier. The Sister passed over the coins and Petie let up her foot to allow the girl to scurry away. She closed her fist around the money.

'Are you coming with me?' Petie urged towards the centre, where Harry floundered, hardly there.

'I need to catch my breath.' Nell leaned against the wall. She didn't recognize this girl in front of her – but she gestured to Petie to throw herself in anyway.

Eight or so feet away, Annie York couldn't stop crying. She was fourteen, looking twelve, small as a pip, squeaky as a gym floor – and all her face was tears. Half-concussed, half-asleep, she was trying to gather some breaths back into her knocked-out lungs. Kerry had scuttled off too quickly, and Annie, gulping fresh breaths, had lost her.

Only now did Annie realize that she'd been duped into fighting for the Kings. Kerry should have believed her when she explained why she wanted nothing to do with those louts. When they strode past the soot-smeared front doors, in their boot-lace ties and black blazers, they grabbed the eyes of everyone – everyone but Annie, it seemed. She was immune: their unpredictability, their pack dynamics and their loud fights unnerved her. She preferred fricassee to the fracas of a late-night brawl; she wanted dates with boys not fights with them. The Kings weren't so bad, she supposed, in her most lenient of moments, but she wanted no part of it.

When Kerry came wheedling down the street, bombarding her with the latest news of a riot in a cinema, a stabbed kid in a dance hall and a fight to end the rivalry with the Sisters once and for all, Annie was more than a little unenthusiastic. She barely looked up from her mother's copy of *Good Housekeeping*. She was even more unenthusiastic about Kerry's suggestion that they should go down and pledge their undying loyalty to the Kings. Annie had asked what benefits she would get, but apart from some waffle about belonging and belongings, Kerry could offer her nothing else. Nevertheless, Annie decided that, if the Kings called on her, she would go, if only to play along.

A flurry of knocks broke the Sunday in half. Kerry plied Mr and Mrs York with excuses, grabbing Annie's arm and dragging her to the brawl in a flurry of excitement. She rolled her eyes, protested, but she grabbed her coat on the way out.

'Shit,' Sal muttered from the edge, while trying to survey the entire Patch in one glance. She saw Somerset fields in her mind's eye, this muddiness, their muddiness. Harry was one-on-three with some Sisters so far in the centre that it was difficult to see her through the mesh of bodies; disfigured in a smash of movement. She was on the ground, then up, untraceable.

Sal watched the fight dance itself out like a creep gone awry as girl took girl in temporary partnerships, limbs protruding, arms breaking the night in random jives.

She backed up until she hit the wall.

'What's wrong, Sally?' Bonbon skipped towards her, raggedy breaths escaping her mouth. Her bottom lip bled from the middle as if cracked from too much smiling and her pale, knobbly knees showed through ripped suit trousers, mud-smudged as a schoolboy's.

'We're going to lose,' Morgan cut in, her cheeks red from fists and the cold.

A King broke through their conversation, closely followed by a Sister. The two smashed against the wall, allowing the Sister to pin the King to the ground. Only a second later, another King battered in and turned the situation on its head and the Sister was on the floor, begging for her freedom.

'There's still time,' Bonbon said. Morgan shook her head, puffing.

'Shut it, Bonnie.'

'It will turn around—' Morgan drew back her fist and walloped Bonbon on the left cheek; she slammed to the floor. Frazzles of ginger hair poked out from the sides of her head like a clown's. If only, as they had sat talking in the penny arcade, figuring out the paths of the future, they could have glimpsed this night – its odd screams, head-butts and punches, skin on skin, lips bursting and teeth spewing, hair skewed at odd angles, crunches, throws, tears, dirt thrown up, rain splashing the foot-stomped puddles – then they might have chosen a different path.

Bonbon sprang back up. She smacked Sal on the arm with a burst of energy.

'Don't have a fighting chance if you don't fight, eh?' Sal nodded. She watched for a few moments more, steadying herself in the cold moonlight.

Harry was using a lighter to inspect a cut on Jackie's head.

'You're fine, Jackie.' She slapped her lightly on the cheek and Jackie moved off. Harry said she was fine, so she was. Her left eyebrow bore a healthy slit, out of which blood had spilled down her face, onto her shirt, her trousers, even her shoes and the ground about her, making marks on the mud.

'We've got them on the ropes, Harry!' Tony laughed while shunting a Sister to the ground, fending off bodies from their bubble. She used the boxing terminology learned from watching her brother at the local club.

'Hold it, we're not done yet!'

Saint pushed through the Kings. Harry grabbed her face, angling it upwards to the lazy streetlight to examine the makings of a scar. A cloud of hot air whispered across the night, the expelled breath of a breathless bunch.

'We've lost some, Harry.' Saint shoved off a Sister trying her luck.

Harry looked around her, taking stock. She noticed some wallflowers missing.

'Where's that kid, the one that was on the floor?'

'Which one?'

'The little one, ribbons in her hair.'

'You mean Annie York?'

'That's the one, she's... she's not...?' *She's not met the same fate as Bernadette.*

'I saw her run off.' Tony looked down, fidgeting. 'She was with her friend from the Terrace when she got knocked down, hard. She wasn't moving. The friend left, and then Annie too.' Tony pointed to the corner.

'Don't worry, Tone.' Harry patted her shoulder with a distracted head looking elsewhere. Some relief in her voice. 'It's her loss.' The Kings itched their necks at the idle dawdle of a police siren threading its way through Islington.

Annie sidled along the wall, hoping to remain unseen and disappear into obscurity as salt dissolves in water. At least she was free, limping along the main road, with its orange lights and route home. As she neared her street, a police car rolled past. It slowed to a stop. After a pause, it began rolling backwards and halted next to Annie. Someone inside cranked the window down.

'Are you alright there, sweetheart?' Annie nodded. 'Hurt?' She shook her head. 'We've had some reports of a fight in this area... gangs. Would you have any knowledge of that? Seen anything like that?' Annie shook her head again. The officers continued talking. 'Okay, well you get on home. It's getting late.' Annie nodded again. The officer mumbled something about a *pretty little thing* to his partner and washed her with his eyes, wetted his lips. Annie cleared her throat. She felt the slam in her chest, her heart still gushing, and went to open her mouth and tell them about the Patch, when the radio blared, crackling across reports. The window snapped up, and the car sped on.

Saint knew the routes and schedules of the local beats. She checked her watch. One would come this way soon.

Through the thick crowd, she weaved towards Harry, the warning on her tongue. The rain slammed harder. Sloppy footslaps echoed around the Patch as the gangs churned up the mud so thick that it greyed the air and wasted the navy sky with a brown tint. The fighters had said farewell to their suits long ago.

When her hand was inches from Harry's shoulder, someone stepped in and slapped Saint away. Her glasses flew into the mud; her vision blurred, she stalled. Her head was ringing, heavy as a border, limbs weighted with shock. She was done for; without a way to calculate herself out of this.

Another set of hands scooped her up by the armpits and righted her.

'Marcus, what are you doing here?' Tony's voice rang out across the Patch.

'Why didn't we get invited to the rumble and tumble?' His speech slurred. Saint thought she could smell whisky in the mud. She reached for her glasses, dirt-smeared and half-bent, and slid them onto her face.

There were ten of them, at least. Spilling onto the Patch like a stain. Tony was shoving at Marcus's chest, to push him off the grass. Reading her anger, Saint assumed that he was the one who had smacked her to the floor and knocked her glasses clean off. When she couldn't snap, Tony did the snapping for her. The Hackers – all of them here – continued to grow onto the Patch; a smirk all over a pretty face. Their bodies pushing in, unrelenting, the long shadows from the streetlights criss-crossing the foot-printed battlefield.

Saint backed up, spotting Harry metres away.

'The Hackers...' Saint said, grappling at Harry's shirtsleeves.

Harry turned to see them, pushing back against Tony. A wave laughing at the sand. She grasped Saint's arm and tugged her towards them.

'Marcus, get out of here. This is *not* your fight.'

'It's between *us*.' Sylvy skidded in from the right. A knife peeped out between her fingers, and everyone noted the flash of it.

'Harry, a copper's coming through here soon,' Saint whispered into her ear. 'His beat, it comes right through, but... I thought we'd be finished before half-past.' The fight pulsed around them – some of the Hackers had already picked fights with Sisters or Kings and Sisters and Kings had picked fights with Hackers, and they were soon caught up in the blur of fists and dirt.

'Oh, come on, Harry, don't be such a spoilsport,' Marcus said. 'We're out celebrating our victory against the Whadcoat lot... we love a good fight. We can teach you girls all about it.'

'I mean it, get off the Patch now, or—'

'You told me to go away last time, but I don't feel like it tonight. This is my turf: it doesn't matter who the hell you think you are.'

Marcus stumbled forwards, trying to fold Harry into his arms. He faltered, she moved, and he fell to the ground. She laughed, stepping backwards – but he grabbed her ankle and brought her down to the ground with him. She kicked, he grappled at her, they tussled in the mud.

Sylvy and Char both took on one of the Hackers, and then Tony piled in to help them, shoving one of them to the floor. Someone grabbed Tony from behind, and Morgan gathered enough air into her fist to deaden a mule and hit him hard on the cheek. In this darkness, it was hard to tell who was on which side, and who was on the sidelines. Sisters fought Hackers and Kings fought Hackers and Sisters and Kings continued to fight around the Hackers, kicking them by accident, skimming the edges of their cheeks with punches. Saint crept backwards, noticing that some of the Sisters had started to scatter as the boys grew more violent, the fight mutating.

And then a yell:

'Copper!' Jackie shouted it for all of them. At the word, more Sisters evaporated down the corner streets, falling in thick streams to the alleys.

A lone policeman ran onto the Patch, holding a hand to his high-peaked custodian helmet, waving a truncheon by his waist uselessly, as if trying to batter the wind out of the air. He tripped across the debris of a fight – broken bottles, discarded handkerchiefs, sloshed footprints – and launched himself towards the centre, where Marcus and Harry and Sylvy still wrestled with each other, neither of their hard skinny bodies competitive or muscular enough to have the final say. Neither knew about the policeman. The twins were pointing knives at one of the boys, slowly threatening him off the Patch with each jab, while Laurie watched on, clapping. Ouisa, too, was kicking a Hacker against a brick wall over and over again. It seemed personal, like she had history with him.

Saint searched the huffing crowd for the policeman, but he had disappeared.

'Where is he?' Saint's voice sailed through the air. 'Where is he?' At her scream, fighters started to lull and stall. All of them looking for the hat, but it was missing. Their eyes dropped to the ground as a small crowd parted, the clusters waned.

A stiletto knife stuck out of his back. His beat had come to an end. Harry stood above him – as did Marcus and Sylvy, their chests charging up and down.

Sylvy still held a knife. Harry did not. A pair of hand-cuffs cracked open lay discarded on the ground. The kids looked at each other, awash with confusion.

They had missed it. Saint had missed it.

'Who...'

'What...'

After silence, questions began trickling out.

'The copper,' Saint's voice melted. The toughness lifted off their skins, leaving that old war-kid fear to shine through. No more than ten of them remained on the Patch.

Harry leaned down to touch the policeman, strangely unafraid of the body's stillness. His pale face shone in the night, the cheeks and jawline dusted with blond peach fuzz. His jacket was newly ironed and the finger clearly ringed.

A siren pushed their still melancholy to panic. The changing tone seemed even slower as the police car rolled onto the Patch and the doors flung open. Marcus and the Hackers raced towards the corner, their shoe-slaps louder than gunshots. Both the policemen took after them, diagonal across the Patch.

Practicality moved her, and Saint pulled the knife from the policeman's back while trying to keep as much distance as possible from the body.

'What happened?' Tony asked, shaking Harry. Tears slipped out of her eyes. Her lips trembled. The word *murder* burrowed into their heads. 'Harry, *what happened?*' She grabbed Harry's shoulders, but she stared forwards, unmoving – the park's new statue, unwilling to rejoin the flowing river of bodies. Together, Saint and Tony pushed her from the Patch, repelled by the sirens, feet travelling quickly over blood-strewn ground. The fighters ran in opposite directions, disbanding so quickly that the police might have been trying to chase yesterday. Everyone grew suspicious of themselves. Victory was inconclusive.

SIXTEEN

The police questioned them one by one. Throughout Monday, lazy knocks rippled along the streets. *Nothing to worry about*, the constable would say, helmet off and cradled against his waist like a toddler with a football. *If you'll come down to the station, we just want to ask you a few questions about last night*. Each King and Sister looked to the floor, searching for their dropped stomach, before reaching behind the door for a coat. Overly polite, outwardly demure, they nodded and followed the policemen into their cars or waited patiently until the time of their meeting and walked through the heavy doors of Caledonian Road Police Station with the confidence of a thousand clams.

The marks from Sunday were difficult not to see. The policemen would reserve comment until sat at the tinny desk opposite the interrogatee. *Some nasty-looking bruises you've got there*, they would burst after a time, no longer able to keep it in. Most of the Kings and Sisters smiled and answered sweetly about some mishap, some accident, some husband.

In their haste to run, the gangs had scattered traces of themselves on the crime scene – a neckerchief, a trampled lipstick, a compact – so the department had to bring them in. After, of course, the Hackers had been trawled through the doors, half of them grassing up the Kings and half of them keeping mum. Marcus named Harry, *that girl in Islington who hit the grandmother with candlesticks*, the one with prior convictions, and the concrete evidence was too hard to ignore. *Persons of interest*, the coppers called it when they stood at their doors. While the signs were clear and the brooches and hairpins strewn across the Patch could pin the crime on them, the detective sergeant, with his stiff brain, his George Medal fastened tight on his breast, still doubted the existence of their gangs. He used words like *involvement, interest, participation*, words that the Kings found easy to avoid with polite, rehearsed phrases… *I don't get involved with that… I've got no interest in that… I don't participate in that kind of thing.*

'I *was* in a fight near Finsbury Park.' Saint pointed to the purple mark under her eye. 'I didn't hear anything about a stabbed copper though. How long will this take? I have to get to work. I'm a typist, you know.'

'I heard something about that.' Tony looked down into her lap. 'I was at church last night helping clear up, you see. You can ask my priest, I was with him the whole time, putting away the communion things. Would you like the telephone number?'

'I heard there was something about a fight, but this is from something else,' Petie said to the detective sergeant, stroking a bluish mark on her left cheek. 'I had... trouble at home.'

The twins had identical testimonies:

'We were both together...' Leslie began.

'Going for a walk—'

'When we stumbled on the fight and got caught in the middle...'

'But we didn't see no coppers...'

'And it ended pretty quickly, so we went home to help with the dishes.'

Harry was one of the last to enter the police station.

'Where were you last night?' the detective sergeant asked. His pen hovered above a blank notebook.

'In The Kings Head, after hours, with the owner. She'll vouch for me.'

'Her name?'

'I'm... not sure.'

Harry had spent most hours of the night and early morning at Saint's kitchen table, where her friend had written up a short script of possible answers. It had been the safest place for them, considering that her parents were away for the weekend and no one would come to Saint's street looking for anyone associated with a brawl near the Bridge. *Tell them that you were with the Crone,* Saint had coached her. *She'll tell them whatever you want. She hates the police.*

'What about Saturday night?' *Then they'll ask you about what happened on the night of Harfleur, if you were involved.*

'I was at the dance hall where the kid got hurt, but we… I…' she slipped, recorrecting herself, forgetting the script, '… had nothing to do with that. I was there to dance with a boy.' The sergeant smiled at sweet, young love. *They like hearing about young couples*, Saint had said.

Then tell them you happened on a brawl or something, like you didn't mean to end up there. Just don't tell them what really happened. That wouldn't be hard; in truth, Harry didn't know what had really happened. The Kings had spent all night appealing to their leader, begging her for answers, for some direction. She drank, she sobered, she drank again and sobered again; she smoked, she breathed, she coughed. She was quiet. When the knock came at her own door later, after she had returned home, Harry had lost herself – somewhere on the Patch, some-where in the grooves of Saint's table. She was confused at the lines on her palm, worried that her own hand had killed a man, more worried that she might never know for sure.

'After I left the pub – and I hadn't drunk all that much – I stumbled on this fight happening, between some gangs… local boys. I wasn't involved in it, and it was practically over by the time I got there, just a few people standing at the centre of the estate. There was something going on, a police car pulled up.' *Don't say you were directly involved, and definitely don't say that you were there.* Harry was off book. 'I heard police sirens and I scarpered. I didn't want to get dragged into it.'

'Because of your previous conviction,' the detective sergeant continued.

'Yes.'

'Could you describe these men at the estate?'

'Tall, dark suits, ducktails. You know…'

'Teds,' the officer completed, nodding. He scribbled down baseless adjectives. He'd got what he came for. 'I think that's all. Thank you.'

It was evening by the time Harry emerged into a wall of mist. Overnight, the rain had turned into a fine spray, clamoured with fog, weather reluctant to run. A sizeable group of Kings had clomped together further down the street near the kerb-parked cars. Some leaned against them, some sat on the bonnets. They talked quiet, smoked quiet, dressed well – orderly, nothing but harmless.

'Made it through?' Saint asked, jumping off the bonnet and strolling towards Harry. 'Said what we talked about?'

'Sort of,' Harry murmured. Her eyes were stuck to the floor. Too soon, she continued: 'Have the Sisters handed it over?'

'Handed what over, Harry?' Tony asked, picking at her nails as she rested her shoulder against the wall.

'The turf? Have they announced their defeat?'

No one answered. They smoked in flat, confused silence.

'But what about the dead copper?' Tony pressed off the wall. 'I thought… I thought it was all over. I thought that we'd forget about the war, let bygones be bygones, you know.'

Harry raised an eyebrow, lighting her own cigarette.

'What made you think that?'

'Because—'

'After all this, bygones be bygones? Bygone where? It was a colossal fuck-up, yes, but—'

'Harry, what is *wrong* with you?' Tony squinted through the night, her fists scrunching and unscrunching. She searched Harry's eyes. 'Bernadette's dead. And now a copper. We can't carry on this bloody *crusade*…' she spat the word. 'It doesn't matter to anyone but us, and it's making matters worse for everyone.'

'Doesn't matter?' Harry asked, recalling Edie's fierce stare, her faith in the Kings. 'I thought you understood how much this matters, to all of us, Tone.'

'I did it for you,' Tony said. 'We all did. But… this has gone too far. The Sisters know it too, and that's why we've not heard from them today. Radio silence on their end.'

White noise buzzed in Harry's head.

'You didn't really think the Kings would last forever, did you?' Tony crossed her arms, smirking. A faint mocking, evergreen sadness behind her look. 'That we'd forever stand up to the boys and run the streets at night. That we'd have the coppers in our pocket and the council in our right hand. What did you think? That if we won, then what? We'd take over from the Hackers? We could be even bigger than them? We could take all of London? What was it that you thought, Harry?'

'It's alright.' Harry scuffed her shoe. 'This makes sense, I guess. You've been looking for a way out for years. I suppose this is finally it. Lucky you.'

'Don't say that, Harry, I don't want to leave.'

'But you will.'

The surrounding Kings pleaded with them to stop, trying to coin the situation into a laugh. Tony, face shocked to stone, looked past Harry's eyes to the wall behind her; to the street around her; the sky.

'It was always going to come to an end, Harry.'

Harry balled her hands and went, in a red-haze moment, to bury her fist in Tony's face. Tony was quicker, and caught her hand before she could land the punch, shoving Harry back into the brick wall. Harry grunted at the impact. Jackie tried to step in but she was held back.

'Did you do it?' Tony hissed, close to Harry's face. 'Tell me, did you do it?'

An empty train clacked across the bridge nearby.

In Tony's question, it was clear: the Kings thought she was guilty. Or at least, they wanted her to be. It would end this dream that had quickly turned into a nightmare, the shaking hands and the shock and the need to follow this leader, unhinged, and unfit to take them any further. But her guilt would also end the feuds and the backlashes that kept them joyously awake and undreaming; her guilt confiscated their streets, stole their midnight hours, relegated the Kings to nothingness. If she opened her mouth and said the truth, *I killed him*, then it would be a disaster. The truth didn't matter.

'No.' She locked eyes onto Tony's, set her mouth firm. 'You know me, Tone. I'd tell you if I did.'

Tony shook her head. She knew Harry better than the others, and knew her well enough to know what her pauses meant. She backed up. *Liar*. Harry had chosen her truth and stuck with it. There was no room for doubt.

257

'It's too far, Harry.' Tony backed off further. It could have been fear in her eyes. 'I can't… not anymore.'

'I didn't do it, Tony. Saint believes me, don't you?' Harry nudged her. She turned to the other Kings, slapping backs and arms and shoulders, pushing spirit into them. Saint cracked under Harry's gaze and nodded, but uncertainty flashed in her eyes, too.

'Sure, Harry.'

'Seems the Kings are on top again.' Harry stepped forward into the crowd. She ruffled Petie's hair. Jackie fell into the celebrations, and the voices started working louder. Some jumped off the bonnet and clattered to the pavement. *Oh come on, Tony, lighten up,* someone said.

Smiles transferred from one face to another, followed by a laugh, a wisecrack, a joke; the Kings had goldfish memories. Murder was an ugly word, and they quickly, willingly, forgot it.

All but Tony, who spun on her heel and walked off into the night, shaking her head.

'Tony…' Saint went to chase after her. Harry held her back, pulled her into the growing storm of Kings.

'She'll cool off. She'll be back.'

Tony had walked away from her before, when she was lying on the floor with the mark of a cricket bat on her cheek, tasting the strong tang of her own blood. Harry had always been certain that she would turn back, but this time she couldn't be so sure. She watched her friend, graceful even now, stride away into the night.

'Would you look at this tripe!' Saint flapped pages of a newspaper in front of Harry. She cleared her throat and performed the article like a newsreader: '*Teddy Boys once more made a nuisance of themselves at Harfleur Hall on Holloway Road last Saturday and Sunday evening. In a brawl between two rival gangs on Andover Estate, innocent girls were caught up in the fracas whilst trying to escape...*'

'What's a fracas?' Leslie asked. Saint ignored her.

'*Trying to escape?* Would it be so hard to believe that we were doing the brawling?' Saint flapped the pages around.

It was much later on Monday evening. The Kings Head had been unthinkably crowded, with windows fogged up and dripping, bar-stools occupied, tables rearranged to accommodate swelling groups; drinks poured, laughs, jibes, and the brawl recounted up to its climactic moments. They added details, embellished, embroidered with cocky snatching phrases and a hundred slurred whisky words. Most of them had since leaked from the pub, and only five were still lingering. Stock remained untaken in the evening air. The business end of a long day's muscled haze. Empty bottles on every surface; tables sticky with dried liquor; ashtrays overflowing – the mess of a grand old time.

Years fanned out in front of Harry like the pages of an unwritten book as she skulked in her corner. Everything was in her hands now; word had travelled to the pub that the Sisters were nowhere to be seen, and Harry had recast the night through the lens of victory.

'There were twice as many of them.' Jackie leaned back in her chair.

'Three times. *Easily*,' Leslie said, while Saint continued to mock the newspaper.

'Sylvy was practically begging for a time out,' the twins went on volleying.

'Practically? She *was*.'

'Too right,' Petie joined in. She sat at the Kings' table in the corner, smoking a cigarette that Harry had given her and Saint had lit. Nell had gone home. Bernadette's funeral was the following day.

'I don't know if I want to ask this...' Saint lowered her voice directly to Harry while the others embellished their tales. '... but what about Ouisa? Have you heard from her?'

Harry inspected her nails.

'You can kiss that opportunity goodbye,' she murmured after a while.

'Right.'

'Dead coppers aren't good for Ouisa's business. Especially when you're trying to get them in your pockets.'

Months of talk about Ouisa had fizzled out like the

end of a firework. Even Ouisa had only been able to give Harry six words when Harry went to Pichetti's on Monday morning to find out what would happen next, full to bursting with questions. She knocked on the door. Ouisa, stood in the back, turned away from Harry, made no move. She assumed Ouisa hadn't heard and walked in. *One more step and you're dead*, she'd said. Harry asked if that meant no. The silence that followed made it clear that Ouisa had no intention of being involved with the Kings.

'Well, do we know how many we lost?' Saint finally relapsed into talk of business, leaning forwards. 'Other than Yorkie and...' *Tony* remained unsaid. 'The Kings who might rat on us, go to the police. The ones we need to watch out for.'

The other Kings had quietened, waiting for the answer. 'How bad is it?' Jackie asked.

Harry smirked, feeding off their gazes. Seconds swelled.

'As far as I can tell... only one.' Curtained thought muffled the room – questions of *who, how*, exclamations insisting that she couldn't be right, surely. *Just one?*

'That's all you, Harry,' Jackie breathed.

'Who'd be stupid enough to turn away from Harry?'

'Who's the one?'

Harry's eyes landed on Petie. 'It's Nell.' Petie held her drink halfway to her lips. Harry continued. 'She was talking to the Crone out the back tonight, followed her into the storeroom. You were all too busy drinking the bar dry, but I got up and went to see what was going on. I stood behind the curtain and heard Nell whispering to her. She said she'd seen me stab the copper. *I bet my life on it*, she said. Apparently, she had hung back when the Hackers arrived, and watched it all play out. She saw me do it, supposedly. She insisted it was an accident, but she still thinks it was me. She's so sure about it that she's thinking of going to the coppers. The Crone told her not to, but she's not the most persuasive.'

'What are we going to do about her?' Jackie's eyes lit up. She had put down her drink. Petie had put down hers.

'Until she does anything—'

'We'd be too late,' Jackie's voice rose. 'We won't know if she goes to the coppers until she goes and then it'll be too—'

'I know her,' Petie interrupted. 'She won't say anything, not yet. Let me talk to her.'

'You would do that?' Harry asked.

'Why not? I'm a King now.'

SEVENTEEN

Since that Monday, Nell had begun to take school seriously. Less messing around, skipping afternoons to shoot
tin ducks in the arcade, wasting the hours until she either
left school for good (a miracle!) or got kicked out. Petie, on
the other hand, had practically dropped out. The golden-
girl-turned-truant rode with the Kings until the early
hours, spending inordinate amounts of money that she
didn't have on clothes, drink, wasted nights in dance halls
– while Nell, still combusting on the inside during waking
hours, put her head down and studied hard. Petie grew
drunk across the street while Nell was busy remembering
orders from Victorian poets, letting her rage shrink into
bare surface nerve.

Neither of them attended Bernadette's funeral. The
affair was small and simple, and Bernadette's parents
had deliberately neglected to share the time and location
with the teenagers. While they had been interviewed by

newspapers and given time to the police's questions and investigations, the parents were reclusive and resigned and too cynical to make a fuss. In the front-page photos – *Parents mourn child killed in Islington stabbing* – they looked sullen, sad, yet peachy, unbothered. They sent their daughter into the next life in an expensive mahogany coffin and then, when the sun rose the following morning, they went to work. It was a Wednesday, after all. There was nothing more to be done.

Two weeks after the brawl, on a Friday evening, Petie paid Nell a visit. *It'll be best, coming from you*, Harry had said, looking right into Petie's eye and down to the bottom of her shoe. Until then, she and Nell had avoided each other on the Terrace, in the arcade, hanging their heads down whenever passing – a nonchalance rigid with effort.

Petie mooched around the corner, checking her hair in the dusty window of a ground-floor flat. She was head to toe in grey, a walking pile of soot. New bruises on her face shone purple-red, ringed with sickly green. Her undereyes lagged heavily, and streaks of make-up peppered her baby-smooth teenage skin. Her hair was curled and piled like Tony's, bleached blonde, her necktie and shirt-collar styled like Harry's; the cigarette behind her ear like Saint's; the twins' clean-cut styling recognizable in the shined shoes, the crisp pleats. Patchwork Petie threw her shoulders back, chest out, full of King-like swagger.

In the distance, Nell kicked around in an empty playground, decked out in scruffy school uniform too small to be comfortable. The playground was all junk. Blitz-printed splayed beams and rafters had been sewn together with tyres and ropes into a soft explosion of kiddie whim and imaginative nonsense where children made entire worlds from rubble. In another life, Petie and Nell had spent many Friday evenings here in the sweet hour when the primary school kids had gone home and the up-to-sixteen-year-olds, those who still played, were the only ones left.

'Bit young to be losing your marbles, aren't you?' Petie quipped, approaching Nell, who was muttering to herself amid the piles of debris. She clambered around the chicken-wire, extra careful not to snag her clothes.

'Maybe I am.' Nell shrugged. 'At least I'd still know how to play with them, though. I suppose you're too old for that sort of thing now. Too busy playing cards with Kings.'

Petie stumbled and twisted her ankle on a loose pile of rubble.

'Need help?' Nell came over with an outstretched arm. Petie swatted her away. 'How's the high life, then?' She looked the suit up and down, assessed the hairstyle. 'You're proper one of them now, aren't you? They even talk about you, Petie, up there with Harry. Bet you love that.' Petie kicked rubble, uninspired. 'Go on then, how is it?'

'Smashing.'

'I bet it is.' Then, under her breath, turning away: 'Smashing windows more like.'

'It's not all tear-ups and trashing—'

'No?'

'No, it's what we do… in between all that. We help each other out, look out for each other.'

'That doesn't sound so different from what *we* used to do.'

'It's more than that, Nell. It's the clothes and the fun… the *fun*. We can go anywhere at any time. On Wednesday, we were in Harfleur all night. We gave the band an extra ten bob to stay for a few more hours and the whole place was ours. Nell, it was the best, it really was.'

'Harfleur…' Nell said. 'You mean the place where—'

'You wouldn't understand. You left after five minutes. You had a taste of it and decided it wasn't for you. In fact, you didn't leave, because you were never even a part of it.'

'Don't be like that, you know why I left,' Nell said, fixing her hazel eyes on her friend for the first time in weeks. 'And we didn't have much choice about joining, did we, really? I don't think they would have taken *no* for an answer. I only joined because I thought it might be fun or it might make me feel like I could be someone or because it might get me away from all this'– she gestured at the dust around them – 'but what I got wasn't exactly what I had in mind, Pete.'

'You were the one who made *me* join!'

'And I'm sorry.' Nell paused. 'Is that why you came looking for me, Pete? Are you mad? Is that it?'

'Harry sent me.'

'Like a letter? Did she stamp you, Pete?' she snickered.

'It's not funny, Nell. This is serious. It's… business.'

'You even talk like them now.' Nell shoved her hands deep into her pockets. 'Business, loyalty…'

'Are you finished?'

'For now.'

'Well, they want you to keep quiet. Saint heard you saying something to the Crone in the Head about going to the coppers. You saying you saw something, you *witnessed*—'

'I *am* a witness. That's how the law works, Petie! You were in school long enough to know that every crime has a—'

'What crime?'

'*What crime*? Harry—'

'You're making it up. Your imagination's running wild because' – she scrambled, breathless – 'because you're jealous of me. Because I kissed Drew, because I'm one of the Kings. But you know, you could've been too, and you kissed that chance goodbye because you got scared. You cried the night Bernie died and you didn't show you had it in you to do what needs to be done to be a King. You barely threw a punch in the rumble—'

'You didn't either! How could you stay with them? After the copper got shivved—'

'You're just jealous, Nellie. You would have stayed if you could, but you're not cut out for it.' Petie lit a cigarette and drew on it long and hard.

'I know what I saw.' Nell strutted towards her, closing the open space. She grappled at the memory's edges: the Patch with its weak streetlight glamour; the hurling bodies of Kings and Sisters and Hackers, dressed in black, brown and grey, throwing themselves at one another with frenetic energy; and the policeman's conical hat bobbing above the others; Harry turning, seeing him, her hand going to push away, a shunt, a flash of silver, Sylvy lying on the floor. The images bent into one in her head. She was convinced Harry had done it; at least, she had convinced herself.

'I thought I was your friend, Pete?' Nell's voice cracked, trailing into a whisper.

'You *are*. Why do you think I'm here, talking to you so nicely?'

'No, you're doing it for Harry. If she's making you do this, Petie... you don't have to. It's still not too late to leave, like I did.'

'It is.' Petie turned away. Her voice was fleshed with a whine. 'I can't leave. I know too much.' She looked at the ground, stamped her foot, reasoning with herself. 'Anyway, I don't *want* to leave. I like it. I like the clothes. I like being listened to.'

'They don't listen to you. They don't care about you at all. We were just there to make up the numbers when others got cut.' Nell's shoulders sagged. 'You're blind.'

'I'm not. I'm seeing how it all works – the *real* world, Nell – clearer than ever.' Petie wafted her arm towards the thickening tide of a late November evening. 'Nell, please!' She chucked the cigarette on the ground to free up both her hands, clapping them on Nell's shoulders and giving her a good shake. 'Please, just keep your trap shut.' Nell's eyes, bulbed with tears, remained fixed on Petie. '*Please* stay quiet.'

'Or what?'

'Or you'll end up like Bernie!' Petie shouted. She sniffed inwards once and strong, and took her friend's arm, holding the wrist with an urgency too tight for comfort. 'Look, you don't even know what you saw. Are you really going to risk *Harry* to have your moment in the spotlight?' As Petie turned away, Nell grabbed at her and they became locked in a strange, jagged tug of war. From some distance, they could be playing a game.

'Look, I *know* what I saw,' Nell enunciated. 'Harry might not even get in trouble, it was an accident, she didn't mean it. She pushed the copper away and...'

Petie pushed her backwards until they were pressing against the wooden slide, a rickety thing that wobbled under the force. The playground buckled under the weight of their conversation. Petie was crying by now, confused by her tears, dabbing and smearing them over her cheeks. 'Just don't, Nellie. You didn't see nothing. You won't say nothing. You won't do nothing.'

'Or you'll shut me up like the Sisters shut up Bernie.'

'That won't happen. I'll make sure it won't.'

'How? You can't tell them what to do.'

'I can, trust me.'

'Then convince them Harry did it, that Harry's the one who *killed*—'

'Stop it! You don't know what you're saying.' She clapped her hands over her ears, suddenly stroppy. When Nell stopped talking, she removed them cautiously. 'What happens if you go to the coppers, then?' Petie tried a new angle. 'Have you thought about that? What would you say? That you were just walking past and saw it all happen in front of you. Or that you were part of it?'

'I'd say that I… was going to find… that I wasn't planning on being there, but I happened across it, and my
friend was—'

'Don't mention me!'

'I'd just say my friend was there and I wanted to help
them out.'

'*And what's the name of your friend*?' Petie put on a
gruff policeman's voice.

'I thought you didn't want me to mention you?'

'I don't, but the coppers will want to know. The point
is, Nell, that you can't say anything without incrimidating
all of us.'

'You mean incrimi*nating*,' Nell snarled.

'The police would want you to pick a story, Nell, and
you'll be sweating under the lights and you'll choose
wrong because I know you, because you do that, and you'll
make up a story which will be wrong because you *don't*
know what you saw.'

Nell chewed the idea in her head. She hadn't thought
that far ahead, Petie saw.

'Please, Nellie… because if I go back to the Kings
and you still go to the coppers, then I don't know what
they'll do.' Nell gawped at her. They were close enough to
embrace like old times. Reconcile, call it off, shake hands.
But the moment passed. 'What is it?' Petie continued
pressing. 'What do you want? Money?'

271

'I want nothing to do with it.' Rashly, quickly, Nell went on. 'Look, I won't say anything to the coppers. Not for you or for your Kings or for Harry or because I don't know what happened or because I'm scared. But because I don't want to put my name on any of this. You're so smart, Petie. You're right. I won't be able to separate *me* from *them*.'

'We're all Kings here,' Petie finished.

'We're not. I'm not. Not here, not anywhere, not anymore. I'm not a King. I came to this decision on my own, alright?'

Kicking off across the playground, Nell left the other girl stranded among the ruins.

'Don't you want to come and have some fun?' Petie teetered after her, wincing as she caught her hand on stray brick-corners. 'It's Friday night, after all.'

'I have things to do. Homework to do.'

'What?'

Nell turned back for a moment.

'Stay away from me, Pete. If I don't get involved, don't get me involved.'

'We live two doors away. We'll bump into each other.'

'And we'll say nothing. You'll go your way, and I'll go mine.' Nell turned her back and began walking away, arms slicing swiftly into the night.

'But Nell!' Petie yelled, with no words on hand to follow. 'Nellie!' She yelled across the playground. Nell, too stubborn to respond, continued walking. 'Nell, come back! It's not funny anymore, come back! Nell!'

Nell didn't turn. She walked away fast, determinedly. Petie stayed a while, shouting at her retreating back, but eventually quieted, moved off, and left the playground far behind.

EIGHTEEN

'The Sisters want to talk terms, not start another fight.' Harry held out her hand. Saint, reluctantly, took the knife from her sleeve and handed it over.

'I'm not letting anything between me and peace,' Saint twittered.

'I can see that,' Harry murmured as she walked over to the bar and stowed the knife behind it.

Midday Saturday, Harfleur Hall was cold and dusky. Someone had opened the curtains that hung in front of the doors and the bright, crisp day elasticated the Kings' shadows across the floor. The mirrors hung empty and figureless, vacant in the foreign daylight. Without its evening glamour, the hall was nothing but piled chairs, cheap floor polish and dust motes swatting around in the stifling air. As Harry paced, her shadow stroked the parquet, covering, then revealing, then covering again, the dark red stain at the centre. Even when Gov, in the future, inevitably made the call to rip up that small section of floor and replace it, the newly installed wooden blocks would remain conspicuously bright – out of sync with the rest of the dance floor.

The Kings had let themselves in through the back door; a concrete block always propping it open, Gov nowhere to be seen. They called the hall theirs now, unofficially or who-gave-a-rat's-ass, it didn't really matter. Harry was long done with those distinctions.

Petie and Leslie rushed in and there were six in the hall: Tony hadn't come back. Saint scolded them for being late, her eyes aflame, hardened. Harry smirked on, puffing out her chest. She slouched, stood, looking as lazy and cool and anticipated as a bank holiday.

Sylvy had asked them here. *She'll come begging for a slice of our turf,* Harry had told them in the Head the night before. *We have it all, and it's our choice whether we give it out.* Tony hadn't been there to tell her to shut up: instead, she'd spoken until the Kings' attention wore thin, the other girls staring hard at the threadbare velvet seating.

The slap of a distant closing door *clonged* through the hall. Someone had removed the block and let it slam. Footsteps – lots of them – getting louder. The Kings looked around at each other, wondering how many legs the Sisters had grown since the brawl.

Sylvy emerged first from the tunnel – and behind her, there was a man. He was stocky, tall, his neck as thick as his pimpled jawline. Sylvy held onto his arm like a vine curdling around a tree trunk. Behind them, another girl with another man, more girls with more men. When it became a question of who led who, the answer was: these were men with their girlfriends. Glitzed up, permed and sweet-smelling, the girls seemed happy just to be there. Holding onto their guys.

The Kings stalled, looking to Harry. Her brow hardened like kilned clay, flat eyelines, her mouth puckered tight. She crossed her arms, leaned back and stuck out her leg, making herself look as unfazed as possible. Her tall attitude shrank; from across the hall, the men dwarfed her. Their arrival, their jostling with each other, threw the hall out of character, and out of Harry's control.

'What's this all about, Sylvy?' Harry shouted across the parquet. Nerves bubbled in her voice, tucking under the vowels.

Sylvy strode across the hall to meet her.

'Vernon's back in London for a couple of weeks on leave. All the boys are. It was a bit… sudden. A bit of a surprise.'

'Well, that's nice, isn't it?' Harry pinned a tight smile to her face. She addressed Sylvy, not daring to look – look up – at Vernon. 'It still doesn't answer why he's *here*, I thought this meeting was between you and—'

'You've turned out to be quite a handful, Harry,' Vernon said. 'I left the ladies in charge because I thought they'd be able to keep the turf safe from the likes of *you*, at least. It wasn't much to ask, but apparently not.' He pulled his arm out of Sylvy's. Her face dropped.

Stomping towards Vernon, clenching her fists, Harry started to argue back: 'You'll be disappointed to hear this but it was easy, Verne.' Harry knew him from school. She knew them all from school. When their bodies were smaller, unregimented, untrained into bulk. He was in his uniform trousers still, which looked strange against his long Teddy coat.

'Was it? I heard something about a dead copper. Or a little birdie told me. You really *have* made a mess while I was away. I thought girls were supposed to do the cleaning up.'

'Sylvy, what is this?' Harry gestured to him. 'What is he doing here?'

'He's—'

'Shut up, Sylv. I think you've done enough damage with your mouth these past few months.'

'But Verne—'

'I said shut it. Let me do the talking for once, huh?' He shook her arm. 'I'm here because Cecil kindly took the time to write me and tell me about all the things you've been getting up to. In so many words, he told me to get on the first boat back to old Blighty and sort it out. *Immediately.* Or the Coshers might be done for.'

'*Cecil* wrote you?' Sylvy's face warped in disgust.

'That little worm,' Harry spat.

'Little worm or not, he did me a bloody great favour. I've even agreed to let him into the Coshers for his trouble.'

'Where is he? Is he coming?' Sylvy looked around, furious.

'No, he's not.' Vernon smiled, amused. 'He was worried what you might do to him when you found out.'

'Rip his head off.'

'Exactly.' Vernon leaned down to her level, like adults do to children. 'Which is why he's in a bar somewhere, drinking his head off instead.'

'It's alright, Sylvy, I'll kill him for you,' Harry said, seething.

'I need to have a word with Harry here, Sylv. Be a good girl and stay quiet for a minute, will you?' Sylvy swallowed and nodded. She met Harry's eyes – not for long, but long enough to show that she realized bringing him here had been a mistake. Perhaps her plan had been to intimidate Harry, but it had gone wrong.

'Edie never made messes like this,' he said. 'Well, not after the first time. But we're reasonable guys. We tolerated her.' He grinned. 'Sylvy told me that you came here to talk terms or something like that.'

Harry nodded.

'Right. Well, I didn't come here to do that.'

'No?'

'No, I came here to take back what's ours. Everything this side of the Bridge right down to the Eaglet pub. As far as I'm concerned, on that turf, there's no such thing as Kings. Edie be damned. She's not here anymore, is she?'

'Verne, I—' Sylvy tried to cut in.

'What did I say?' Vernon snapped. His voice echoed around the hall, amplified. Sylvy shrank back.

'Leave her be, Vernon,' Saint edged in.

'What if I say no?' Harry asked.

'No?'

'We won the turf, fair and square, in a fight.' She turned to Sylvy, trying to restore some order. 'Sylvy, we *agreed*.' Even to her own ears, her voice sounded thin, pleading, high.

'Let's stop this nonsense.' Vernon shunted Sylvy away from him. She nudged against their group, and played the shock off her face with shrugs, grasping hands with the other girlfriends. He peeled back his dark coat and revealed, tucked in his waistband, a shining Luger pistol. The version of this meeting where the Sisters and the Kings tussled over which street their turf ended on and who could do deals where, and what was what and how it worked, fell away; their rivalry shrank to grains of sand on an endless beach.

He eased the pistol out of his waistband by the polished hilt, slowly, and waved it towards the Kings. Most of them ducked, some whimpered, making Vernon and the other boys belly-laugh. At a lag, the girlfriends tittered.

Harry had not moved an inch.

'That's enough of your games. I don't know why I'm asking you this. The turf is ours, sweetheart.'

'Why are you here, then,' Harry taunted, 'if it was never ours? Sounds like you're asking for it back, to me.'

His brows crunched together. But whether he couldn't, or didn't want to, work it out, he swung his arm up and aimed the gun at Harry's head.

'Call it good manners, then. Give it back, Harry. The lot.'

She stepped towards the shining barrel.

'No.'

Vernon took a step forward, with the gun still pointed out at her. The gap between the pistol's nib and the skin of her forehead narrowed.

'They taught us how to use these in the army,' Vernon continued. Another step forward. 'I've used them. And I'll use it again unless you get back in your place. Give it back.' She remained still, her soles sewn to the floor. He stepped forward once more, until there was no air left. The circle of the barrel touched her forehead. 'I'll give you until three.'

Sylvy made protests near them. The Kings were silent, frozen.

'One.'

'I won't.'

He pressed the gun on her harder, confused that she didn't buckle and crumple like paper.

'Do you *want* to die, Harry?' he shouted, spit on her face, level pegging with the gun. She didn't reply. Tony would have pulled her back, she thought. Told her *he's not worth it, don't bother,* and dissolved the situation. Vernon gritted his teeth, small fear now threading into his eyes. 'Two.'

'Harry, just let him have it,' Saint pleaded from behind. The twins joined in, their voices melting into one another. 'It's not worth it.'

'Listen to them, Harry.'

She stood her ground. Vernon pressed in closer, readying his hand to squeeze the trigger.

A loud *clunk* from the gallery pierced the silence. Vernon looked up, loosening his grip. There was nothing and no one there behind the railings, but his pause was long enough for Saint to lunge forwards, push against his arm and send the shiny pistol singing across the floor. It skidded across the parquet, across the ghostly dark-red stain, across their shadows, and came to a stop, nuzzling Sylvy's shoe. Her eyes wide and unbelieving, she bent down and plucked it from the floor. It was heavy and impractical, dragging on her hand.

'C'mon, baby. Hand it over.' Vernon stretched his palm towards her, patting it with his fingers like an owner training a dog. 'Don't be stupid, Sylv. You don't even know how to fire that thing. You'll probably shoot yourself in the foot with it.'

'Sylvy, don't.' Char shook her head beside her friend. 'Not to him.'

Sylvy locked eyes with Harry, lifted the gun – and aimed it towards Vernon. He watched on, unmoving.

'What is it that you want, then?'

'To see the look on your face.' She closed one eye, as if lining up the shot. 'And the turf would be nice. The girls' turf. Kings, Sisters, doesn't matter, but you've got to let us hang about on it, on *our* terms, in our own gangs. Yes?'

'No.'

Sylvy sighed and with some enjoyment, pinging off Harry's grin, aimed the gun to the side of Vernon's head, and squeezed her hand around the trigger. A muted *click* echoed about the hall. Sylvy closed her hand around the trigger again. The same noise tittered from the pistol. Silent, she lowered the Luger and glared at Vernon – who was already building into a laugh.

'You didn't really think there'd be bullets in there, did you?' Vernon laughed. The other boys laughed too.

'There's plenty of guns around since the war, sweetheart, but not the ammunition to fill them.'

Sylvy gripped the pistol – fireless but no less powerful – tighter and started to walk backwards. Vernon, confused, asked *what the hell* she was doing, but she carried on reversing – then turned and started to run. The other Sisters followed, and the boys, hot on their heels and yelling possessives.

'You're done, Harry.' Vernon turned back to her, pointing in her blushed face, while Sylvy made her getaway. He started to back up while talking. 'This little game of yours, it's over. You're right, I'm not sure why we even asked for the turf. It was never yours... and it was never Edie's.'

'Get her name out of your mouth!' Harry shouted. 'You didn't know her.'

'Sure I did.' Vernon smiled. 'It's a shame what happened to her.' Harry went to chase him, but her friends held her back.

Before she whipped around the corner, gun still dangling from her hand, Sylvy turned and held Harry's gaze. An apology, a confusion, something forever unresolved in her eyes. All that fire, all that burning, all for nothing.

Earlier that afternoon, Harry had walked her streets alone. The fog had released the city from its grip hook, a night of rain washing it out. She had patted Petie's shoulder as she crossed her on the stairs and ploughed onto the pavement. She shook hands with Roddy as he opened the Rink. She crossed the Bridge without a destination in mind, an arrowhead spilling through space. The shops had seemed to ripple open, the penny arcade jingling invitingly. She steered clear of the Patch and the police station, but soon, sooner than expected, her revolution was complete.

There was to be a meeting at the Dent. The Kings were to discuss the future and what would happen next. As she approached, her Kings were not there. Instead, she spotted two vans parked on the road. In white paint, on the side of the bottle-green vans, read *Norris Construction Company*. The collected dust of new buildings smeared the sides.

'What's going on here?' Harry asked herself. She quickened her pace. Four men – some burly, some slender, all dressed alike in homemade woollen jumpers tucked into high-waisted trousers – stared back. 'What's going on?' Harry asked.

'What do you think, sweetheart?'

'Take a guess.'

Harry could think of nothing to say.

'New contract. There's to be a new post office here, and a couple of flats on top. A few months for it to go up and then it'll be like it was there all along.'

'But… you can't.'

'We can, darling. Council's orders, I'm afraid.'

'Why are you sad to see it go?' The tallest and burliest asked. 'It's a heap of rubbish. No use to anyone.'

'But...' Harry began. 'How can...' she began, again. 'I don't...' She stuttered and stalled and kicked her tongue against her teeth in the hopes of getting the motor started. But it was dead. Harry shrank before the burly builders with their hammers and drills and swirling cones of cement pouring foundations over the rubble and soil. Beams had already been ripped down, ready for replacement with tree-fresh wood, honey-pine-smelling, lying carefully in the open back of the van. It had only been a morning, but the Dent was unrecognizable. Its troughs and holes had already been patched, cemented over.

Tony, 2017

We talk until the light falls and the corners of the pub start
to fade. No one else turns up for the reunion, but it doesn't
matter – everyone is already here. Between our wrinkled
hands, among the napkins and glasses, Harry stands to
make her stand to the Sisters and speechify about scars and
suits, and Petie is saying *too right* somewhere off to the
right of the table, a cigarette between her fingers; the Sisters
are outside the window and Sylvy is grinding her teeth like
a greyhound ready to slip out the gates. Even the policeman
takes a turn on the table. November 12th was a long day.
Neither of us dare to say to the other, *it was Harry, right?*

As we talk about rides in cars and our stupid mess of
knife flicks, leg flicks, finger flicks, I forget about the sign
on the door – 'CLOSING SUNDAY'. At some point, the
football match comes to an end, someone turns the televisions to silent, and the men filter out. The sun sets on the
garden outside, bathing our stories in dusk-light.

Saint starts to ridicule me for my cynicism. I would expect nothing less.

'I know, I know, we'll forget this the second we step out the door, *blah blah blah*, waste of time.' I laugh and mock her for looking at her watch; she taps her nail on its face and says, 'I should probably head off.'

I nod, and we move towards the door, joints popping as we stand. We thank the bartender, who pauses explaining his heart-line tattoo to a customer, and salutes us like troops shipping out.

Lingering on the doorstep won't do us any good. I could look back and see the paisley carpet and the fake mahogany and try to rinse memories out of it, but it's been too long. Before we leave it behind completely, Saint looks back inside, which gives me permission to do the same. Then her eyes flit to me.

'It was nice to see you.'

'Likewise.'

'Remember this, Tone.'

'I will.'

There's space for us to talk about next year, but we don't. Perhaps we'll have another reunion somewhere else, or perhaps this was the last. Perhaps this is the last time I'll come here. Perhaps we'll never see each other again, or see another November 12th again. It's not important now, anyway.

KELLY FROST

Time feels impossibly urgent when you're young. I've become more liberal with endings and beginnings. With a career of breaks breaking into nothing, nothing nearing something until slumping back into nothing again, I've learned the two are often interchangeable, opening onto one another. There's the familiar drabness that comes with memories, the droop when the napkins and the glasses are cleared away. I would be lying if I said there wasn't some comfort in it too, that reminiscing ends only to begin again somewhere else, with someone else; our memories door-stopped so that other kids can learn to make them. Our history, contorted through the years by exaggeration, is amorphous and unreliable, vital and alive, a slippery thing found in odd shoulder-bumps and favours between girls.

I reach out for Saint's hand, holding it for a moment.

'Thanks,' I tell her. She knows what for. Patting me on the arm, Saint leaves to walk her way, leaves me to walk mine, the same pavement stretching out beneath our feet.

The last of the afternoon's rays reflect off the café fronts as I walk back to the station. A show-off sun resists its setting. The streets look good like this, all bathed in orange.

Blocking out the rays here and there, some kids cross the road to the other side, comfortable in their gaits, hands shoved into pockets, striding as a pack. For a second, in this light, it's us: Petie, Saint, the twins. Close enough to touch if I cross the road.

We had to grow ourselves out of expecting Harry to show up, like it was a bad habit. Keep ourselves from asking when she would swing open the door and stride in, because the pub seemed incomplete without her. As if a building could be incomplete without a person – like a roof tile missing.

She got caught, in the end, of course. Not for the policeman's death, but for the random crimes she threw herself into afterwards. Paying for it in her own way in unchecked self-sabotage; her dreadful heltering and skeltering from one theft, one drug-trade, to the next. She worked with Ouisa for a while, I think. Petie fell in with that crowd too, both of them holed up in the back of some dirty club on Tottenham Court Road, counting stacks of paper under the glare of an Irish boy, fingers stained with the purchases of others. Her sentences lengthened, the gaps between them shortening, and she was never on Blackstock Road long enough to make any claim on it. The boys would never let her. The girls fell apart without her. With the Kings gone, she figured that she might as well make herself disappear too, and committed to her own erasure, blending into a mob at the riots near Notting

Hill. She found herself serving four years in a now-disused prison. Complications from pneumonia – not even the disease itself – killed her, before the sixties had even come and gone.

Jackie told me all this at one of the first reunions before we reached the front of the queue for drinks. She said there had been murmurings of a funeral procession ending at The Kings Head, but no one stepped in to arrange it. No invitations were ever sent. I prefer it that way; funeral processions mark an end – but Harry was eternal. No coffin was good enough for her.

At every swing of the door, our heads still turned just to be sure. None of us would have been surprised if she'd strode in and declared it time to get going. When she wanted us to find her, she would be there. Reappearing on cue. Waiting for us in a stranger's handwriting, in the slick curves of a *g* or *s*, even in the messy apostrophes – or the gaps between letters, where apostrophes should be.

I have believed for decades that my step into uncharted waters was mine and mine alone. More than that, I wore it as a badge of honour, as the made-good girl, sunglasses-clad, knowing I was the one who made it out from Wells Terrace, the one who really made it. It was my face that made the model agency track me down through the newspaper and call me, and I had chosen to say *yes* to the woman on the telephone, and I had chosen to stand on the rafters and pose with my feet at right angles from one another, hands shoved in my pockets, wearing a net hat that I had chosen at the tailors.

I see now that's not the truth.

The more I dwell on that night we parted ways outside the police station – and truly, I never saw Harry again after that – the more my certainty softens. She had been excessively cruel that day when she spat at me *you've been looking for a way out for years*, pushing me away with both hands and venom in her eyes. Shunting me out.

But if it wasn't for those shunts, I would have stayed. I would have waited with her for the downfall, the riots, scooped up for crimes committed to waste time, afraid to leave, committed to *staying put.* And in those first months after we fell apart, I was grateful to be out – out of Finsbury Park, out from under Harry's thumb, out from the dark park where moonlight shone onto a stabbed back.

Harry suggested that I dyed my hair platinum to bring out the paleness in my cheeks. She chose the net hat at the tailors, her eyes lingering on the doily, and I wanted it because she wanted it. I stood like that because it's how she stood. She was the one who staged that photo, who took it; she was probably the one who developed it and sent it to the newspaper office. It terrifies me, thinking how much control she had over my life. How relentlessly she cared.

I wanted to pretend that my choices were mine alone, but I can feel Harry in the echo of all my decisions, even now. We're all still carrying out her plan, performing our roles.

Typical Harry, to have a debt hanging over my head. I owe her my life.

ACKNOWLEDGEMENTS

I'll start with huge thanks to my wonderful agent, Ciara McEllin, for taking a chance on me, and my editor at Atlantic, Joanna Lee. Ladies, your patience, guidance, and dedication have helped this book – and me – to grow in so many ways.

Publishing is a team sport, so I would like to thank James Roxburgh and everyone at Atlantic who has worked to create a final package that I think we can all be proud of. In particular, thank you to Sophie Walker and Laura O'Donnell for their passion and creativity, and to the designers for putting together a cover which is better than I ever dared to imagine. Thanks also goes to Sarah Chatwin, who made me question why writers dread the copyedit so much, and to all those who had a hand in typesetting and proofing this book.

Most journeys start with brilliant teachers, so thank you to all my English teachers and tutors, especially Mr D. and Mr H. Thanks to the Romilly Road gang – Sarah,

Sam, Alasdair, Auguste, and Blake – for the memories of Finsbury Park, and to Katie, an honorary member, for her indispensable advice. Thanks also to my friends and colleagues at the *Jersey Evening Post* and *Bailiwick Express* for their support.

It feels odd to thank the photographers who have no idea that I spent hours poring over their work, but I send my gratitude anyway to Sir Don McCullin and Ken Russell. Their everlasting shots of Finsbury Park gangs and the Teddy Girls inspired 19-year-old me, who found them so painfully cool, to seek out a nearby notebook and start putting a version of their lives to paper.

A special thanks, also, to Joseph O'Connor, whom I admire, and who reassured me that this book had legs (and for the tip about including the photographic material in my submission).

Finally, to my family. I am fortunate enough to have parents who let me find my own way – and were there to give me confidence when I lacked it in myself. To them, for everything, and to my amazing big brother, Sean, who I aspire to be like every day. And to SB.